THE PURPOSE OF VENGEANCE

A Vampire's Story

JADE LINDSAY

ACKNOWLEDGEMENTS

To my son, Harrison. I came up with the idea for this story while I was pregnant with you, and now it's yours. Also to my nanny Pauline, for your unwavering love and support.

DISCLAIMER

This work of fiction has not been vetted by a professional sensitivity reader, so I hope that any descriptions or word choices cause no inadvertent offence.

CONTENT

Part One: Carlos

Prologue, Chapter 1

Chapter 2, Chapter 3

Chapter 4, Chapter 5

Chapter 6, Chapter 7

Chapter 8, Chapter 9

Chapter 10, Chapter 11

Part Two: Ailana

Chapter 12, Chapter 13

Chapter 14, Chapter 15

Chapter 16, Chapter 17

Chapter 18, Chapter 19

Chapter 20, Chapter 21

Chapter 22

Part One: Carlos

Prologue

The year that I died was 1864; I'd turned twenty three only five months prior.

Dispute was rife in Spain, as Queen Isabella the second hurtled closer to being usurped from her throne - by her own son, no less - a heatwave swept the nation at the beginning of June, and whispers throughout the streets of Sevilla were of the war and little else.

I seldom glimpsed those rays of sunshine, as I lay in bed riddled with an awful disease that had spitefully elected to steal any form of comfort I had in my simple life. There was so much yet to experience and even more to live for; it was a cruel fate indeed to know I was destined never to see it come to fruition. My father tended to me around the clock; he never said as much, but I'm sure he feared I would pass away if he ever let me out of his sight. This night would turn out to be quite different. Father left earlier in the evening, and had so far not returned.

I laid helplessly in bed, propped up on a mound of pillows coughing up all but my spleen. The moon threw dazzling white rays into my room as it slid between thin layers of scattered clouds, and one constant reminded me of the world outside my aged window pane, in the form of clattering, clopping horse hooves and the creak of carriage wheels trundling past.

A small comfort. At quarter to eleven father returned, accompanied by a gentleman I had never before seen. This man was the strangest person I had ever encountered, or would ever encounter thereafter.

I can still recall a myriad of details from that night, despite my illness, and I doubt if I'll ever forget them. He wore genuine Italian leather boots, a well tailored suit of deep maroon and had only a thin layer of facial hair adorning his sculpted cheekbones.

Though it was shorter than the fashion of the day, I thought it only served to make him look more attractive. Dark brown curls hung freely about his shoulders, and two catlike green eyes evoked an incomparable feeling akin to being frozen in the fixed stare of a predator.

I found myself captivated, mesmerised by each fluid, effortless motion he made.

"Good evening ... sir."

I wheezed, lifting a trembling hand for him to shake. This fellows skin was cold as a cadaver; I forced myself to suppress a shiver as he tipped his top hat forward by way of a greeting.

"Good evening to you, Carlos Fernandez. I must say you were right Gustavo, he does not look at all well."

He addressed my father but didn't take his eyes from me. Father came forward wringing his hands together, looking quite mad as he hung on the stranger's every word with bated breath. Clearly, this man's opinion meant a great deal.

"So what do you think Señor, will you take him with you? Will you save him?"

Father's words took me by surprise; I had no idea he had been making plans for my future without me.

"What do you mean by that, father? Is he a foreign doctor? Am I expected to ... travel? I really don't think I could bear it in my current state."

"No son, not a doctor."

He murmured, looking at the ground and wringing his hands more heavily.

"You know we can't afford that, not even with what your mother left us."

It was then that Señor Roberts, the pale white, cold man turned slightly in his crouched position to look at him.

"Would you rather I take it from here?"

Father nodded vigorously.

"My name is Gillian, young Carlos, that is what you may call me from now on. I have met and spoken with your father a number of times and I believe we can both benefit from each other if we cooperate."

He spoke in a blunt manner, yet his tone was light.

"What is it ... that you want?"

I rasped, with a great deal of effort.

"Your good father has already been quite plain about the fact that you are his nearest and dearest and would do anything - even betray your God - to save you. It just so happens that I have plans to travel and have been searching for the perfect companion. But first I must ask ...what is your true understanding of death?"

He spoke so casually of such a dark matter that at first, I was disposed to think he was cruel. It soon became apparent, however, that he was uncommonly familiar with the subject and not altogether uncaring.

"I believe death in this life is a gateway to the next, either to God or to Satan."

I replied, though my voice was wafer thin and cracked in my throat.

"You are right," he told me "to an extent."

Gillian stood abruptly and took to slowly pacing up and down my bedside.

He produced a cigar from inside his pocket and lit it with a match, such a swift gesture as it struck the grazed edge of the box from whence it came, that I almost missed it.

"A cure is what I am offering you. It requires you to die, therefore you would pass through the gateway. You would not be rid of this world, however, you would return but in a state far removed from anything you have yet experienced. All I need is your consent to go forward."

He revealed his white, pointed teeth in a dazzling grin. I for one, could not see how this made any sense.

"I'm sorry sir ... I don't follow."

The man let out a bark of a laugh and gave me the kind of pitying look one might give a confused child.

"What if your death was the key to the rest of your life? What if your untimely demise made you stronger than you have ever been? What if you could look as young and handsome as you do today, forever? If I told you that you could go on living for another five hundred years, or more, without even having to think of dying, what would you say if I could offer you all of that?"

His eyes sparkled with excitement in the light of the gas oilers as he leaned forward, gaze keener than a bird of prey's. My mind reeled as shock permeated my body in waves. I looked to my father, who had been watching Gillian and I converse in silence. He gave me an encouraging smile.

"What exactly are you saying? Are you a messenger from God?"

"Actually, I'm completely the opposite. If you choose to accept my offer of immortality, you understand there would be no going back?"

He looked for all the world as if he made a habit of visiting people on their deathbeds to offer them eternal life. I couldn't fathom why father would push me to settle down, then encourage me to abandon my life for a new one instead of greeting death like a good Catholic.

"Son, I know I have never been able to offer you much in this life, but I think we both know you are capable of so much more."

"I cannot simply just…leave you."

"Please," he beseeched me, "take this opportunity. I shall make sure Anne is looked after as long as you promise me one thing."

I sighed, weakened by the weight of the evening and the conversation, along with the magnitude of my illness. I was tired of this.

"Pray tell, father, what is it you wish me to do?"

"Promise you will make the most of Señor Robert's offer and do not give up until you find your purpose, son. Find your purpose and fill your life with it, promise me?"

A fit of coughs took over and when Gillian thumped me on the back, flecks of blood flew onto the bed sheets. After I had regained composure, I spoke to them; my broken voice was barely more than a whisper.

"Okay I'll do it, I accept your offer. Just make it quick."

Gillian's smile stretched from one ear to the other, like that of a babe's who'd been told Christmas would arrive early.

"Excellent! If it's any consolation, I plan to compensate your father with a substantial monetary gift before I leave this place, young one. He will live out the rest of his human life in comfort."

He stubbed his cigar out and placed the remainder inside his jacket pocket. I watched with morbid curiosity as his sharp canines pierced the skin of his wrist, drawing thick blood that was blacker than night itself.

"You must drink this, then I'm afraid I will have to bring your death forward to now. Do not fear, you shall reawaken and when you do, that is when our journey will begin."

I obliged to drink the blood that spilled from his wrist; it was a potent liquid, the likes of which I had never tasted. My head spun and I allowed the delirious sensation to take over. I'd had but a few gulps when he took his arm away; as he wiped the blood from his wrist I saw the wound was already healing. I turned to my father one more time before Gillian dealt the final blow.

"I love you father. I will make you proud, though I shall miss you terribly."

A single tear rolled down his cheek into his black moustache, and he smiled with the warmth of a thousand memories.

"I am already proud of you son, I just want you to be proud of yourself now."

Gillian placed his hands either side of my head, then he spoke the last words I would ever hear with my mortal ears.

"Welcome to the legions of the undead, brother Carlos."

With a sharp movement he twisted his hands, severing the spinal cord from my brain.

Chapter One

1869; Five years passed between that fateful night and my return to Spanish soil. Salty sea air cloaked my body, as fond and familiar as a smile from a long lost friend. I surveyed the docks below from the shadows on deck, breathing in and out through my nose for the sole necessity of identifying danger.

I watched the progress of the men unloading our belongings; with my new sight, even the most drab colours morphed into dazzling displays, tiny insects became discernible crawling amongst the leaves, and I could count each loop of cotton threaded in the clothing of my comrades.

Chirping crickets called to each other over the beating hearts of the city's residents, but I remained silent as crewmembers emptied the sturdy, sea bearing vessel which had been my home.

Gillian's gallantry towards the humans was, as always, unrivalled. Single handedly, he carried forty boxes of goods from the ship before handsomely paying a gentleman to go ahead to our destination with the luggage. *La Mansión Junto el Agua* was a huge estate that Gillian had designed and built for himself on the river banks of The Guadalquivir.

It was his pride and joy; if memory serves me he spent the better part of twenty years building it, and only finished construction two summers before we met. I'd hoped that upon returning to Sevilla, after many long years at sea, I might feel some form of contentment. During my travels I'd often thought of my last night alive, and the final conversation I'd had with my father.

His plea that I make a life for myself was always there in the back of my mind, reminding me to fill my days with purpose or risk no longer being of any use.

Gillian and I had visited Germany, France, Switzerland, England - even the far frozen reaches of Transylvania - where the locals seemed more inclined to believe my mentor and I were not all we seemed. They had given us a wide berth and we repaid the gesture in much the same way. I was sure that hearing of these adventures would've pleased father, just as well as I knew an incredible emptiness plagued me from dusk until dawn.

I was missing something, yet I had no idea what it was.

"Why must you look so forlorn, young Carlos? I thought you would be pleased to return to your home soil."

Gillian stated, joining me as I reached the bottom of the steps. He could never find out I'd been discontent, so I hurriedly arranged my expression to appear untroubled.

"I am much pleased, Gillian, though I admit to feeling rather weary after our long journey and would appreciate a drink."

His deep red lips broke into a wide grin that showcased his pearly white fangs; he slapped me on the back in good nature, keeping his arm firmly around my shoulders as he led me down the cobbled path.

"Come then, we must drink. It just so happens I sent word ahead of our imminent arrival and hired a room at the nearest bar."

Once our luggage had been carted away, Gillian took us to a tavern called *El Cansado Marinero*. It was a small, crooked wooden building on the outskirts of the docks filled with loud, intoxicated people. He led us through a patchy fog of cigarette smoke, and jostling crowds enjoying a romantic melody played by a live guitarist. A young flamenco dancer accompanied him; her hips swayed in sync with the music and threw her dress into a flurry of red fire.

We didn't stop to enjoy the festivities; Gillian marched past the bar, where I caught the eye of a stranger leaning on the counter. He was sitting on an overturned beer barrel, strongly giving off the impression he was up to something. His dark skinned face was marked with tiny craters, he had a single gold hoop through one ear and a short, bristling moustache of black and grey.

His eyes lingered especially on Gillian's back as he disappeared into a private room separate to the main tavern. By the time we were sitting at our table and I had my first sips of red wine, I'd already forgotten him.

"I've been thinking, it might be a rather nice idea to properly celebrate our return to Sevilla, in the style of a banquet. What are your thoughts on the matter?"

I met his eyes for the first time since we'd sat down, then I thought over his words. I'd always sought to avoid social situations as persistently as Gillian sought to be involved in them, but I had never been the one out of us both that usually got their own way.

"I think that would be quite fitting, Señor, as would another glass of this -" I checked the label on the bottle "- oak matured tempranillo, it's exquisite."

Gillian fixed me with a look as he refilled my glass.

"I must seek out some young men and women to attend then, my guests will go thirsty otherwise."

And so it was, that after we'd emptied two bottles of red wine, we made our way to the main bar to mingle. Gillian busied himself talking with two young people, whilst I opted to watch the guitarist and his wondrous dancer. She really was breathtaking; gold and silver bangles adorned the smooth, brown skin of her wrists, chiming like the sweetest bells each time she twirled. Henna tattoos decorated her bare feet, they depicted graceful flowers under threaded cotton ankle bracelets.

The music faded into the background until it felt like the two of us were alone; I watched her dance, her chocolate eyes twinkled and her curly black hair wafted the scent of fresh cut flowers towards me.

"A coin, señor?"

I realised the melody had come to an end, and the woman stood before me holding out a top hat.

"Oh of course, may I ask the name of the talented dancer?"

Her smile was genuine, it radiated an aura of pure goodness and warmth; I dropped two gold coins inside the hat.

"Its Maria, and *muchas gracias*."

She winked, then walked away to collect from the other patrons of the tavern. It was then I remembered my sire who was, predictably, at the bar with a crowd of admirers under a haze of raucous laughter.

"Come Señor, we've done nout but drink alcohol since we docked. It's time to return to the mansion for some *proper* sustenance."

I said, approaching him and the group he'd drawn. His eyes found mine in a dangerously blurred manner.

"Yes, Carlos," he replied in a slur "you are quite right. Who among you wishes to donate some blood, and learn more about vampires?"

A few hands shot up in response.

"Gillian, I must insist you keep your voice down!" I hissed, steering him towards the door.

A blast of warm air hit us as we stumbled through the saloon doors; two girls and a young man followed behind, whispering excitedly to each other. I hung back as Gillian proffered each an arm, then led them in a zig-zagging line up the uneven, cobbled street.

I wanted to be quite certain we were alone. I gave one last, sweeping glance over the dock yard. There, under the protective shadow of the bar's jutting roof gutter, stood a motionless figure. The metal signpost overhead squeaked eerily with each gust of wind. Whomever it was did not move when they saw me looking, which I found most unsettling; after only a moment they turned away and disappeared beyond a street corner, like a cloud of smoke scattered by the single swipe of a gloved hand.

Turning up the collar of my overcoat, I pulled my hat a little lower to cover my eyes and made haste to rejoin my sire and his companions further up the path.

Chapter Two

La Mansión Junto al Aguá sat on the south side of the great, running river. Its numerous arched windows loomed over all who entered, preceded by a long, white gravel pathway twice as wide as any street and tall modern gas lamps were set at intervals of ten metres, which threw a warm blanket of golden light over the lawns.

The property was hidden by a thicket of lush greenery and guarded by an impressive circle of towering palm trees. Bird of Paradise and Cannas graced the borders, drowning the night with their intoxicating perfume. I craned my neck to get a good view as I followed my sire towards the house, filled with a joyous sense of contentment to be home.

Inside, it was exactly as I remembered. White stone walls were decorated with paintings of the natural world, marble tile ran underfoot and the hand rails which bedecked the double staircase, like every other piece of furniture in the house, had been expertly crafted by deft hands from pine.

Each corner, chair leg or swirl was cut just so and everything was kept polished; the house gleamed under Gillian's rigorous, daily inspections.

My stay here five years ago had been horribly disorienting, but thankfully very brief. It was directly after my sire had dug through the newly laid soil to find my coffin, ripped off the lid and pulled me up into a crisp, sparkling night. I hadn't much chance to get acquainted with the idea of being undead, before

Gillian then packed us up to go and sail upon the tameless seas for several years.

I walked past his study on the way to my room, the smell of cigars and whisky seeped from under his door and I could almost hear his thoughts whirring as he paced. How eager he was to surround himself with admirers, drinks and tales until the nights were given over to sunrise, inevitably forcing us back into the shadows.

*

By the end of our first week back in Sevilla the mansion was once again filled with housekeepers, stable boys, farriers, gardeners and cooks. They worked tirelessly each day to make certain our home would be ready to receive guests. On the night of the get-together, a palpable buzz of nervous excitement gripped the household staff and myself, but none more so than Gillian.

A square package had been put in my room during the day, wrapped in brown paper and tied with string. Upon opening it I found a mottled green dinner suit, with a matching bow tie and top hat. Knowing immediately who was responsible for this gift, I was not one bit surprised when I noticed the new pair of shoes that went with it. No expense had been spared; they were made from the finest black leather, thoroughly polished and burnished dark brown.

I trimmed my beard into a neat cut and got dressed, then headed out to meet Gillian on the landing. Two potted parlour palms in gold, baroque-style pots stood at the head of the bannisters where he waited. Needless to say he looked finer than even myself, in a maroon velvet suit and matching top hat.

In what I could only assume was a statement of rebellion, he'd tied a pink chiffon sash to the base of his hat with a decent sized bow showing at the front. His leather boots were a pine brown with burnished rims like my own.

"I must say you look quite dapper this evening ... I wonder who could be behind that?"

He looked me up and down then patted me heartily on the shoulder. I smiled, humoured by his pretending not to know how the suit and shoes came to me.

"Muchos Gracias Señor, so do you, but that is not unusual is it?"

We descended the stairs and stood by the front doors, which had been left open for guests to come in.

I stood silently at Gillian's side; he heartily shook hands with vampires and humans alike, before letting them pass through so they could roam the smoking room and the dining hall as they pleased.

"Quite the turnout don't you think?"

He smiled with a unique charm whilst observing the slowly filling lobby. I found I could not answer his question with as much gusto as he'd asked it.

"You've done a marvellous job. Your guests will be quite pleased, I'm sure."

Two green eyes, like a leopard's, turned sharply onto me; his dark curls bounced as he turned his head. To think I could have fooled him was folly.

"I'm not entirely satisfied that you're invested in this, you know. What have I missed, Señor Fernández? What displeases you?"

I cleared my throat in a pointed manner, blinking against a sudden, warm gust of wind.

"There is some kind of...something feels wrong, Gillian. It's quite difficult to put into words but, I can't escape the feeling that something's amiss tonight."

His smile vanished into thin air; he inadvertently allowed two guests to pass through the doors without a greeting.

"I do hope you are wrong about that."

He murmured. I couldn't help but notice his thick brows crease together with worry.

Back inside, the guests had gravitated towards a small, live orchestra which took up the whole far side of the dining hall. The current song was one of Bach's, Gillian's favoured composer; they played a haunting yet beautiful ballad that made the guests sigh.

Beyond that was an extremely long table, arranged around which were forty or more chairs. The catering had been made to accommodate all guests; set upon the table were five whole chickens, dressed and displayed alongside dishes of roasted vegetables and goblets of donated blood.

"You could make more of an effort to look like you're having a good time, you know, it won't kill you."

Gillian muttered in my ear, sidling up beside me as I stood alone watching the progress of the guests.

Humans and vampires alike were laughing and talking together, sipping from silver goblets or else having a private bite in the secluded corners with someone willing.

I looked at him then with what I hoped wasn't a grimace, but as he rolled his eyes I knew I had failed.

"Go and speak with people, they will be thrilled to hear of your first trip outside of Spain."

He suggested. I'd been keeping my senses on high alert for any trouble, but there would be no getting out of Gillian's request so I obliged to give it a try. I shared polite yet extremely banal conversations, I nodded and smiled vigorously without ever feeling wholly united.

After enduring all manner of trivial talk, my sire called for silence in the dining hall. Every person looked up from what they were doing to gaze avidly at

Gillian; he received their attention with a dazzling, white toothed grin.

"I would like to officially welcome you all to my home. I hope you are enjoying the orchestra and the food, for which our thanks must go to the revered, resident cooks. They have been working day and night for the last week, preparing the wonderful spread you see before you. Tonight, we honour the long awaited return of myself and my young protégé, Carlos Fernandez -"

He gave a small bow in my direction, which was followed by a smattering of polite applause.

"I invite you to tuck in and-"

At that moment, we were interrupted by the doors of the hall being thrown open, and a clan of unfamiliar vampires entered.

The man at the head of the group was somehow familiar, but I couldn't place my finger on why. He had a gold hoop earring in one ear, a pock marked face and a bristling moustache. After a moment of pondering I finally remembered where I'd seen him. It had been in the tavern, at the docks on our first night back in Sevilla.

Gillian's mouth was reduced to a thin line, his eyes had turned hard and cold. His stare held the intruding clan at bay, as if an invisible wall of brick had been placed in front of them.

He did not take kindly to being interrupted, so I sincerely hoped these vampires had a good reason behind their untimely arrival. The stench of dirt and blood unfurled from them into the air, infecting the guests with fear like a toxic gas. I found myself captivated by the same sense of foreboding which had filled me earlier, as Gillian finally addressed them.

"Your names please, if you would be so kind as to provide them." He demanded.

Their leading man did not move, nor show any inclination towards a smile. His sunken black eyes simply bore into Gillians; the minutes trickled painfully by, until I felt sure they would not resume speaking.

"My name is Raoul."

The vampire said eventually, with a voice rough like desert sands and a foreign twang I could not place.

"Though perhaps, you might have heard my other title? My comrades also know me as The Red Wolf, which is the literal translation of my name."

Gillian raised an eyebrow, seething with scepticism.

"I've never heard of you. Is there any particular reason why you barged into my home unannounced and stopped me in the middle of a speech I was giving?"

Raoul scowled, possibly irked by being talked to like a naughty child interrupting an adult conversation.

"My clan and I thought you might explain to us why we didn't receive an invitation to this little get-together, I've been led to believe you welcome all supernatural beings, as well as the human faction."

"Well, as I have never heard of you I assume that is why you never received an invitation. If you wish to stay, drink, talk and mingle - you're welcome to do so - as long as you adhere to my rules."

The two vampires glared at each other; it was an unspoken battle for dominance watched on by a crowd that all held their breath, waiting for a verdict.

"And what rules are they?"

"You will not drink from anyone unwilling, bring harm to or kill any human, nor will you venture into any out of bounds areas of the house."

The room breathed a sigh of relief simultaneously. The rivals stood motionless, some greedily stared over the scene in the room, waiting to get stuck in.

"We accept your rules. My second in command, Jameson-"

Here, he gestured to a thin vampire with dirty blonde hair and a hook nose protruding from between two, piggy blue eyes.

" -and his assistant Peter-"

He waved a hand towards the rather large vampire on his other side, who sported jagged yellowed teeth and an air of malevolence.

"-will be expecting to sit next to me, if it can be arranged."

Gillian smiled tightly and bowed, without taking his eyes from Raoul.

When he straightened up, he clapped his hands together. The housemaids brought extra chairs to the table and soon, uneasy conversation resumed within the hall whilst the guests took their place at the table and began to tuck in. I watched Raoul's henchmen take a seat beside their leader.

The one called Jameson had a cold glint in his eyes, he drank in the scene before him with a thirst that made me uneasy. He wore a calculating look that suggested he'd made a mental note of every aspect of the room; all the exits, potential strengths and weaknesses of those within the four walls.

I presumed he would file this information away for later, to exploit at his will. A shiver trickled down my spine when he turned and caught sight of me watching; I moved a hand consciously over my beard, breaking eye contact to look at his friend.

Peter was guzzling down a goblet of blood and had several more pulled up around him on the table. He clearly had none of the brains that his superior, blonde colleague had. The wide eyed look of glee with which he gawked - almost salivating - at the human guests, led me to conclude this man would be the muscle in any heinous, dastardly plans that Jameson or Raoul could possibly think up.

After each belly was full and the alcohol was flowing freely, Gillian announced that everyone was free to move about the halls as they wished, with exceptions to the upper floors and the gardens. In the midst of the hub-bub and movement, he took the opportunity to pull me aside.

"I do not trust this Raoul fellow one bit."

He told me, puffing on his cigar like they were going out of fashion.

"I mean to say, if he is as notorious as he claims I would surely have heard news of him before now."

"Perhaps you can use this opportunity to do a bit of detective work."

I suggested. He nodded vigorously and put an arm around my shoulders to pull me closer, until I found myself drowning in clouds of smoke which rose over us in spirals.

"That is exactly what I intend to do, my boy. I will have a more in depth conversation with Raoul, but I would like you to keep an eye on that blonde, Jameson, and his brutish friend. I would be altogether happier knowing they in particular are being kept track of while I'm otherwise occupied."

I agreed wholeheartedly; yet once he'd left to seek out his target I found myself in the dark about the whereabouts of my own. I glided amongst groups of people for a while, then I spotted them vacating the male restrooms. Keeping a good distance, I watched them talk privately behind a potted fan palm, which was at least as tall as they were.

They didn't notice me; alongside the drunken babble of conversation, music and constant movement, I had little hope of hearing their discussion. I'd managed to glean a few snippets of harmless gossip about the other guests, when somebody jostled into my shoulder as they walked by.

My thoughts scattered; it was a young woman with dark brown hair. She turned back and smiled, so I nodded politely as she walked away. Those few seconds were enough for me to lose sight of my targets; when I returned my attention unto them, they were no longer hiding behind the houseplants.

"*Dammit.*" I muttered.

I surprised myself, as usually I didn't curse aloud. I turned on the spot but couldn't see Jameson or Peter.

There was a change in the air. A warmer draft was blowing in and upon inspection, I found that the doors leading to the back gardens had been left ajar.

The gardens were off limits, which meant one or more Gillian's guests had broken the rules. I knew no good would come if I left them unsearched, so silent as an owl, I disappeared through the door and made my way across a small room with a double set of glass doors on the other side.

Opening them, I stepped into the humid night air to investigate.

My heart slipped into my stomach, as I was greeted by a most familiar, tantalising scent on the breeze - one that set my throat on fire with thirst when it was in the air. Blood, however on this occasion it wasn't to be pursued to satiate my hunger, but to be mourned.

The amount I could smell was sure to lead only to tragedy, still I followed it to the end of a short maze of neatly cut bushes. The broken corpse of a young lady was sprawled across the patio pathway; blood still leaked from a vicious neck wound and ran over her skin onto the cold slabs. I got stained with it as I collapsed to my knees and leant over her, hoping I might be able to identify the poor wretch.

Her skin had turned stone cold and her eyes stared blankly towards the heavens, unaware her lovely ball gown had been ruined or that the pins keeping her hat on were coming loose. She had been human, whoever she was. My sire was going to lose all responsibility for his actions upon hearing of this audacious act.

Two rules had been broken, one of them a most sacred rule. The perpetrator would pay for it, sure as night turns to day and we were all forced back to the coffin.

Chapter Three

Gillian was as I'd predicted, mortified.

"You mean to tell me Carlos, you did not catch the culprit?"

"There was no one to be seen when I arrived, it was deserted. Did you manage to get any information from Raoul?"

"He didn't give much away, but I'm sure he intends to settle here and challenge my authority in Sevilla."

I watched my sire's every move with apprehension. His face was unreadable; he'd barely looked at the body since I showed it to him and now he stood before me, surrounded by our guests looking as if he might very well strangle somebody.

"Search everywhere, check all the rooms and make sure nothing else has been disturbed. I cannot see that Raoul or his clan are still here but I want to be sure."

He said. I searched every room to no avail, all the while thinking that if I hadn't allowed myself to be distracted by that young woman, I wouldn't have lost sight of the two henchmen.

Gillian made an announcement shortly thereafter, asking his guests to leave early so he could retire for the night. It was nearing three in the morning when everyone finally traipsed out through the front doors, making their way to the carriages.

*

In keeping with the rest of the building Gillian's study was large, with a high ceiling and windows dressed in heavy burgundy drapes. Thick, emerald green carpet lined the floors and the furniture was hand carved from polished pine.

A glass fronted cabinet stood tall next to the window, it housed Gillian's whisky and cigars which was as vast and varied a collection as any I'd seen. Flames crackled and popped in the grate of a white stone fireplace; the intense heat danced over my pale skin as I stared into the light with my hands clasped behind my back. All manner of thoughts befuddled me whilst Gillian silently looked over some papers at his desk; the ever present sting of hunger in my gut reminded me I hadn't drunk a single drop of blood the whole night.

Eventually, he stood up. Turning to the window, he stared into nothingness wearing that unreadable expression he so favoured. He held a cigar as was his custom, though he'd smoked double his usual amount after the harrowing events of the evening. He swilled a tumbler of amber liquid in his hand as he finally spoke.

"I simply cannot fathom the meaning of these events, Carlos."

He announced. I looked away from the fireplace, but still he had his back to the room whilst he surveyed his gardens through a small gap between the curtains.

"My guests have only two rules to follow; don't kill or take unwilling blood from humans and respect the household - ergo - if I say somewhere is off limits I bloody well mean it. Is that so much to ask?"

He turned his head then and looked me directly in the eye. One of his thick, dark eyebrows had curved high into his curly fringe.

"No, I don't think so."

I said honestly. There was a moment of silence. My mind wandered back to blood and Gillian came to stand next to his desk once again. Out of the blue, he slammed a fist down on the smooth surface of the table, causing a lamp to sway precariously.

"I will find that Red Wolf's lair and burn it to the ground, then we shall see which of us is the better at disrespecting the other's territory."

So absorbed in his thoughts was he, that I was sure he'd forgotten I was even there. Once again I was reminded of my thirst by the intense burning in my throat.

"I would like to go out and hunt, Gillian. The confinement of these four walls is too much to bear at the present time."

He raised a bushy eyebrow, confused, taking a minute to process that my request had nothing to do with what he'd been talking about.

"There are a number of humans staying here for the night, why not take one of them for a stroll in the gardens?"

I linked my hands behind me as he topped up his tumbler with more whisky.

"Please sir, I need to get out of here and gather my thoughts. Besides, I would prefer to find my own meal."

For the briefest moment I thought he was ignorant to my plight, as he lit up another cigar and took a swig of alcohol.

"Yes, very well. You may leave, but be sure to return before dawn."

Without another word I left the room and the tense atmosphere behind. Taking the stairs two at a time, I dashed for the front door.

*

The night air had a calming effect on my nerves. I was infinitely more at ease under the moonlight, as if I'd finally shed a stuffy jacket.

I navigated the sleeping city via the rooftops, jumping and falling freely from one to the next as the sound of beating hearts pervaded my ears from all angles. I hoped to find someone wandering in the streets, as I knew I couldn't enter any home without an invitation now.

As it was, there were plenty of despondent souls that did not have a home at all, making their life on the cobbled pavements with nothing more than a holey, threadbare blanket - in some cases not even having that. I had no wish to take their lives.

Five years had passed since I'd joined the legions of the undead, but Gillian had made learning self control very easy. I would take some blood, heal them using a drop or two of my own, then erase their memory of the interaction with hypnotic suggestion and soon thereafter left, repeating the process until I was full.

Just as I had decided to turn in for the night, the sharp echo of raised voices issued from the streets below. I halted mid pounce and dropped onto a deserted balcony to see from whence the disturbance came. It was the unmistakable racket of a man and woman arguing. I focused my hearing to catch their words.

"You stupid girl! You are always making messes for me. I am not well, you torment your poor father!"

There was a sharp slap as his hand crossed her face, then something stranger.

"Why must you always hit me father, there is no need. I'll clean my messes, go back to bed before you wake Josiah and Eleanor."

A door banged open and a woman came stumbling out of it, obviously having just been thrown.

"You are a waste of space and time - a complete and utter shame to this family!"

A man appeared in the doorway, cussing at the young woman before slamming the door in her face.

"And you are a miserable old man, as always!"

She shouted at the aged wood. I watched in silent wonderment as she brushed the dirt from her skirt and began to gather something at the front door.

I'd forgotten about returning to the mansion; so struck was I by this woman's fierce, unwavering refusal to back down that before I could further contemplate, I leapt from the balcony and landed soundlessly on the pavement. I approached in silence from the shadows.

"Excuse me señora, do you require assistance?"

The woman jolted with surprise and whipped around. Her eyes were a soft brown and grew wide as she looked me up and down. It was then I realised I'd already met her before; that night in the tavern her dancing had held me captive. She held a hand to her chest and closed her eyes briefly before replying.

"Thank you, señor, but it's 'señorita'. I am not married."

"My apologies, Maria."

She gave me a quizzical look, then recognition crossed her features as it had mine. I stepped closer to feel the heat radiating from her body and she smoothed down her skirt, brushing crumbs of dirt onto the floor.

"Of course I remember you señor, you were the only person who couldn't take their eyes off me that night."

She smiled, then picked up a crate of cut flowers and started walking in the direction of the river bank.

I fell into step beside her which she didn't seem to mind, and we made our way down a narrow cobbled path lit by the occasional gas lamp. Laundry hung on lines criss-crossing above our heads whilst black mud crawled over our boots - in her case dainty slippers - so it was impossible to walk without squelching.

I was inadvertently reminded of my human life; how my father would turn his hand to most any profession he could in order to scrape together some money. Being cooped up in a filthy space day after day, with never a rest from the neighbours' comings and goings was a life I wouldn't wish on anyone, least of all this beautiful young woman full of spirit who had her whole life ahead of her.

"Well, if we are to stroll together I should at least know your name."

She said, after a few minutes of walking.

"My name is Carlos Fernandez, I apologise for my lack of social skills, it's not often I spend time with young ladies as pretty as yourself."

"You're sweet, Carlos. I haven't had the pleasure of speaking to such a well mannered man in a long time, this place is so dismal and frequented only by poorly paid, frustrated merchants. I run a stall at the market near the river selling cut flowers from my garden, but I dream of leaving this place behind to go and discover the world. Do you not find the repetition of misery here tiresome?"

Her eyes lit up as she tilted her head to stare at the starry sky, apparently lost in an imagined world of her own.

"I used to," I admitted, "but I've done a lot of travelling recently, so I'm glad to be home in Sevilla."

She gasped in surprise and almost dropped her crate.

"You've travelled! Where?"

"I visited Germany, France, Transylvania and Switzerland, but only in the briefest sense, not for pleasure. My si - er, employer - had some business to attend to and asked that I accompany him."

Maria listened, enthralled by my story. Her bosom heaved in delight under her sweet smile.

"Amazing," she said. "truly."

The lapping of water at a bank nearby reached my ears. The sky was now a shade or two lighter, which meant that dawn would soon be upon us.

I had forgotten myself, and the time. Gillian would no doubt be consumed by irritation if I stayed out for much longer.

"Forgive me, Maria, but I'd quite forgotten the lateness of the hour so, if you wouldn't mind I must be off."

I told her, attempting to hide the hint of regret in my voice. She looked at me full on; it was as if she were staring into my very soul.

"Thank you for your company, Senor Fernandez. It's been the most delightful experience I've had in quite some time, talking to you."

"Please, you may call me Carlos. It has been a pleasure talking with you too, Maria."

I took hold of her hand and brushed my lips against her soft brown skin. She shuddered as she withdrew, clutching her arms around her box of flowers. As she made to walk away, she hesitated and turned back.

"Forgive my forwardness but, I can't help noticing you're extremely pale for a Spanish born man."

Her eyes were large and expectant; If I were alive my heart would've skipped several beats.

"Well, yes. I stayed indoors for the majority of my childhood due to sensitive skin, that is why I go for my walks in the moonlight; the sun has long been my enemy."

I lied. Though the thought of deceiving the poor girl was regrettable, all the same I hoped she accepted it.

"I should hope that doesn't stop you from visiting me again." She replied. "I would like that very much."

We shared one last smile, then left to go our separate ways.

My spirits soared as I committed to memory Maria's silky black hair, chocolate brown eyes and the sweet aroma of her skin. Darting from one balcony to another in the direction of my home, I swelled with undeniable satisfaction. I realised, with a little surprise, that I couldn't recall ever feeling so happy.

Chapter Four

As the sun fell below Sevilla's jagged rooftop horizon the following evening, Gillian knocked on the door of my bedroom.

He was accompanied by a human with blushing skin and copper hair; he wore a stern look that forced his thick eyebrows into a downward slant over his eyes.

"Carlos, this is Genevieve. She's kindly volunteered to donate her blood this evening, should you wish to indulge."

The girl smiled expectantly, clasping both dainty hands behind her. I closed my copy of Les Miserables and rose from the small wingback chair I'd been reading in. Internally, I squirmed with discomfort at the unnatural nature of such a thing.

Though I was well versed in controlling my instinct to kill, I always preferred to venture out at night to find my own source of blood. However, to refuse this offer would be considered disrespectful - that was far more disconcerting a notion.

"I thank you for your generosity, if you wish, you may sit on the bed whilst I talk privately with my sire."

I told the woman, who nodded and went to make herself comfortable.

"You will need your strength for the excursion I have planned tonight."

Gillian said quietly, leaning closer.

"When the two of you are finished, meet me at the entrance. Bring your revolver and cloak."

With that, he left the room. I turned to address the smiling woman who had out a pen knife and a goblet. She talked happily as I drained a cup full of her blood; I bit into my wrist and offered her a few drops to staunch the bleeding of her superficial wound.

Once I was satisfied she'd healed and my goblet was drained, she wandered off to the drawing room and I to the entrance hall, laden with my cloak and gun as instructed.

I hadn't the foggiest clue what Gillian was planning, and he did nothing to eschew my puzzlement as we headed out the door. Rather, he foisted upon me a case of wooden bullets and bade me follow him into the night.

*

"He has been here, I can smell it."

We were perched delicately on the roof of an old warehouse building, at the old abandoned section docks.

I breathed in a lungful of air, but most odours on the breeze were monopolised by the stench of sea brine, and I could only detect rusting metal from the skeletal structures surrounding us. These were the last surviving monuments of what once housed the finest fish packing business in Spain.

"Follow my lead and keep your revolver ready."

Gillian murmured, loading his pistol with patented wooden bullets. We dropped from the rooftops to the ground, silent and quick like field mice. A swathe of clouds slid in front of the bright full moon above, as Gillian followed his nose and I him.

After a few minutes of navigating the corridor of pathways twisting left and right through the ruined buildings, he held up a fisted hand to signal for me to stop. I too had seen the shadowy figure flit across the space some fifty yards ahead. Whomever it was, they darted into the yawning mouth of a corrugated metal warehouse with no doors.

Gillian gave a silent nod, signalling that we should follow. We became invisible in the shadows cast by disrupted moonlight; not a single noise did we utter as we moved to close in on our target.

I took another deep breath; what greeted my senses almost saw me abandon the plan and rush ahead, for the stench of human blood was overwhelming. Gillian had smelled it also; the worry upon his face had certainly not been there before. Our pace quickened and we entered the building.

Gaping holes in the roof where the structure had rotted allowed streams of moonlight to penetrate the large space and thick dust covered the abandoned corpses of once fine machinery, which littered the edges of the room.

Alas, our eyes were drawn to one thing; bodies hung from what remained of the ceiling - twelve in total - each suspended from their bleeding, broken necks by industrial chains.

Their blood stained the floor in macabre puddles beneath them and the wall directly behind was daubed in it too, fashioned into a symbol of a wolf's head. It was this morbid calling card that caused my stomach to turn above anything else. Gillian didn't look horrified as I surely did, his expression was simply grim. Perhaps because he had not been there to accost the villain himself, perhaps he wished he had not been too late to prevent this awful occurrence.

"It seems we've missed the opportunity to catch Raoul, this time around."

He stated, his tone forcibly stoic as he stared at the mark on the wall behind the dead humans.

"This was an act of defiance, intended to draw my attention to the fact I am no longer the only vampire in this city with ambition. He is mistaken, however, if he truly believes this kind of behaviour will place the crown on his head."

Gillian turned away from the gory spectre; apparently he had seen his fill.

"What Raoul forgets, Carlos, is that violence alone does not a powerful vampire make. It is instead, age and experience. I have lived for five thousand years, his entire lifespan is but a mere spec upon the pages of my own, personal journal. Sooner or later we will meet and he shall regret ever thinking he could be king in this city."

"Fine words Senor, fine indeed. But I must ask...are they in danger of becoming - "

" - like us? I cannot be sure at this point, only in time can such things be known."

Suddenly, another body emerged from the shadows and moved to stand in the entryway.

With immortal speed, I raised my gun and clicked twice to cock the patented bullets into place. Before I could act further, Gillian held up a hand to stop me.

"Who are you?" He demanded.

"You know who we are; my name is Jameson, I am here with my accomplice, Peter. We came to represent The Red Wolf."

A second man, discernable due to his large size, now stood close behind wearing an evil grin.

"Give me one good reason why I should not allow my young apprentice here to shoot you both in the heart where you stand."

Gillian growled, taking a step forward as Jameson moved closer also. Each clack of his heeled boots echoed sharply in my ears.

"If you wish to challenge Raoul for control of the undead community, he requests you gather whatever forces you have at your disposal and meet with him on this night a week from now, on the side of the river nearest the cathedral. That is, if you can find any vampires. Does not the company you keep, comprise mostly of human women?"

Jameson taunted us with a light chuckle that set Gillian's teeth grinding in his head. My sire managed to bite back whatever retort filled his mind, replying instead with sickening politeness.

"You would be surprised how many allies I have accrued over my long life. What are the rules of this hypothetical battle?"

"There are no rules."

"There must be rules," Gillian refuted "or else there is no order. I say no weapons made of wood, we are not looking to kill each other. In their place, I suggest the first to concede grants fealty to the victor. Give me a week to write to my fellows and in the meantime, I suggest you advise your ring leader to take down these bodies and dispose of them. We don't need to draw attention to ourselves in this way merely to prove a point, or we shall each of us find ourselves burning at the stake. Tell Raoul I look forward to proving who is the true king and who is not."

Gillian's smile was colder than a brick made of ice. Jameson tipped his dirt covered fraying top hat, then like a breath of wind, both he and his accomplice vanished.

I lowered my gun and stowed it away; Gillian took a cigar from his pocket and began to smoke. He almost seemed to have forgotten me as he wandered forward, staring up at the starry sky absorbed in thought.

"It looks as if we found what we were searching for, does it not?"

I questioned, joining him in the open mouth of the warehouse.

"Far from it, Carlos. Our search has only just begun ... here, have a cigar."

He passed me a smoke along with a box of matches, yet my own thoughts had strayed away from the abandoned docks. They flew to a poor neighbourhood near the river, where a beautiful woman sat in poverty.

It was a place far from warring vampires and murder, a place I longed to be more than anywhere else in that moment.

Chapter Five

Upon the roof of the house opposite Maria's, I waited. I waited until her father stopped shouting, until the sounds of his blows and her pleas died down, until all I could hear were her anguished sobs.

It was then I proceeded to pounce onto the balcony outside her window where, through a set of sheer curtains, I could see her. A single candle was lit on her bedside table top; I called to her softly.

"Maria."

Her sobbing ceased at once and she looked round with a start.

"Carlos, you came back!"

She stood and ran to the window; her brown eyes were rimmed with tears, which she hastened to wipe away and replace with a beautiful smile.

"I was beginning to wonder if you had forgotten me, you know."

"How could I possibly forget *you*? I've brought something I think you'll like."

I withdrew a small object wrapped in cloth from my pocket, and handed it to her. She unwrapped the gift, but her eagerness was somewhat marred by puzzlement.

"What is it?" She asked.

"It's a slice of fruitcake soaked in rum. I dare say you have never tried such a thing?"

She beamed in delight.

"No, I haven't."

"Then by all means, enjoy it, for it is all yours."

Maria wasted no time in breaking off a piece of the succulent treat. She chewed slowly; a myriad of expressions crossed her face as she discovered new tastes and textures. She savoured each sticky, sweet bite as crumbs fell into her exposed cleavage. She didn't speak again until every last bit was devoured.

Maria closed her eyes whilst the last piece slid down, then she licked her fingers clean.

"By God that was the most ... incredible thing I have ever tasted ... thank you Senor."

"Por favor," I said in earnest "you may call me Carlos."

"Carlos ... "

She repeated my name slowly, rolling the syllables on her tongue as if it were something foreign, until once again a smile dominated her lovely features.

"It so happens that I too have a gift I wish to bestow. It was clipped from the communal garden this very morning."

Maria went back inside for a moment or two, then she returned with something in her hands. It was a blood red carnation, with such an intricate design of petals that I couldn't help but marvel at its breathtaking beauty as I took in my own hands.

"Thank you Maria ... I will treasure it for its entire lifetime."

I promised, with sincerity such that we could both feel it. I met her warm gaze and held it in my own; we stayed that way for what seemed an hour or more, but it was only a moment or two in reality. When Maria spoke again it was with some hesitation, or perhaps nervousness.

"Would you like to come inside for a moment? You may warm your cold hands, for I am sure they must be freezing."

I considered her offer; how joyous it would be to surround myself with her scent like a swaddling blanket, to see the interior of her room which held intimate details about her life.

"Carlos? I apologise if I caused any offence."

My eyes had glazed over in the time spent daydreaming.

"Forgive me, Maria, you have done no such thing. I've merely remembered that I am here without notifying my brother. He will not be pleased by my prolonged absence."

I inwardly chastised myself for the falsehood; though it was nought but a small lie, it was a necessity I would rather dispense with. The agonising pangs of hunger still burned my veins; thus far I had managed to suppress it but sadly, I could hold it back no longer.

The time to say goodnight had come far too quickly.

Maria looked crestfallen, so I placed a hand on her shoulder and hid my embarrassment when she shuddered from the cold. I got caught in the gaze of her twinkling eyes, and my own slipped down to her pink lips. I found myself falling forward, we were so close I could have lost myself in her warmth.

"Who is *that*?"

Maria said aloud. The moment splintered into a thousand hypothetical shards at the whisper of danger; I peered down at the cobbled streets below, only to catch the last wisp of a stranger's cloak disappearing beyond the corner at the street's end.

"Regretfully, I must leave you now, Maria, so I bid you goodnight."

I forced myself to leave her with a promise that I would return, then, pocketing the red carnation, I leapt from the balcony.

"Be safe, Señor."

She called out. I pursued the alley down which the mysterious figure had escaped; I was faced with an empty, cobblestone street of old houses and dirt covered porch arches.

"Were you looking for me?"

I turned about quickly so the hem of my cloak whipped against my shins.

The smooth voice had issued from a shadowy corner at my back. There wasn't time to orient myself before I felt a hard jab to the back of my head; so forceful in nature was the blow that it knocked me to the ground.

With a feral hiss, I put out a spurt of supernatural strength to propel myself onto the top of a brick wall close by, then twisted to face my attackers, a snarl escaping from deep in my throat.

"I don't know who you people think you are, but I assure you - "

"Do you not recognise us, young one?"

As I looked on, I realised I did. One was quite large and the other rather skinny, with oily blonde hair pulled into a ponytail. My frown deepened further still.

"What are you both doing? This area is part of Gillian's territory, you have no business being here." I spat.

Peter the giant showed his yellow teeth; he gnashed them together in a threatening manner, but I refused to succumb to their intimidations.

"We were simply looking for a tasty morsel or two, nothing more. I apologise if we were ... encroaching at all."

"*Or*, perhaps you are once again at work on some vile machination. These parts are *my* hunting grounds."

The words may have been more possessive than I would normally allow, but I had no choice but to mark this place as mine if I hoped to prevent any harm coming to Maria or her family.

"Goodnight, Señor." Jameson murmured, tipping his frayed top hat.

"We shall endeavour not to wander this way again; Lord only knows it's so easy to get lost around here."

With one last evil grin, they blended into the shadows of the night and were gone. I relaxed my stance and jumped down, taking a cigar from the inner fold of my dinner jacket.

As I walked, I puffed smoke into a haze that lingered about my head, whilst my thoughts strayed to Maria.

How vulnerable she would be if Jameson and Peter continued to frequent this place. It was an abhorrent notion, and I promised myself I would not allow it.

Chapter Six

Over the next few days, I saw little of Gillian.

He remained sequestered in his study and only emerged when he had written a handful of letters. He hired a youthful, thin gentleman cursed with blemishes upon his face to deliver them on horseback.

We began to receive house guests from across the globe in almost no time at all; twenty or so vampires now resided within our walls, but none were more captivating or mysterious than the lovely Carmen. Her movements were languid and effortless, her skin was white and smooth as alabaster stone, her eyes chocolate and her ringleted hair like swirls of molten caramel.

Gillian's chivalrous tendencies magnified tenfold in her presence; they spent several hours together secluded in the gardens, and although she appeared to enjoy his affections she wielded the singularly unique power to resist his shows of flattery.

The evening before we were to do battle with the red wolf's clan, Gillian invited each of us to the drawing room. Tiled floor from the entrance and lobby gave way to thick emerald carpet, cabinets and small nest tables cluttered the room's edges, and handsome wingback chairs upholstered in fine ruby red were arranged in random formation throughout the middle.

When I pushed open the heavy pine doors, twenty unfamiliar faces stared back at me; a stern looking woman in a silver kimono that was secured at the waist by a blue silk obi, raised a judging eyebrow as she tapped ash from her cigarette.

A Brazilian man that I did know, whose name was Marcelo, wore a tall green feather in his hat. He gave me a curt nod of recognition and I returned it with a small bow; Gillian had introduced us at a port in Germany, where I was shamefully beaten by them both in numerous card games. There was a woman from Athens that I did not recognise; she could barely manage a single word of Spanish, but smiled warmly and curtsied when I came to introduce myself.

It wasn't long before the man in charge arrived; his demeanour was calm, but his smile was tight and the corners of his eyes pinched, betraying his masked tension. Without him having to speak a word, the room fell silent and each eye was on him in expectation, not that there was much conversation happening anyhow.

"You all know why I have requested your presence here tonight. This city, my home, is beset by miscreants that have no qualms about exposing our species to the human world. Raoul wishes to overthrow my peaceful leadership and so, we are obliged to answer the call to battle."

Not a sound was issued in response to this statement, each vampire stared avidly at Gillian as if each syllable he spoke was precious.

"In their selfish quest, many people have gone missing and the humans are starting to notice."

He withdrew a copy of our local newspaper from the inner folds of his gold embroidered, maroon coat, the heading of which read thusly:

NUMBER OF MISSING LOCALS RISES INTO THE HUNDREDS

Below were illustrations of a number of the victim's faces, a few of them I thought I might've recognised. Marcelo took the newspaper to read up close.

"It is likely these people have not just gone missing, but have been turned in order that our enemy's ranks may grow, but alas, it is we who have the upper hand in our combined experience and of course, my secret weapon."

Gillian said; he tapped the end of his nose in a conspiratorial manner; at first I hadn't a clue what he was referring to, until I recalled a time when I was newly turned and he had revealed to me a little of his past in a particular conversation.

Before he turned five thousand years ago, Gillian had already been blessed with the gift of magic. His father was a shaman and so passed on this gift to his son.

I knew not the details of his experience, only that some couple of hundred years after his death my sire made the decision to suppress his other side, functioning not as a hybrid of the two species, but as only a vampire.

"The final matter I wish to discuss is the one time waiving of a personal household rule; should any of my human donors express a desire to join the legions of the undead, grant them that wish. I advise you not to do so lightly, however, since the progeny you create will remain your responsibility once we return to our own lives. I look forward to seeing you all again on the other side of victory."

His words echoed as the double doors to the dining hall opened in perfect synchronicity. The humans Gillian did spake of then entered, each dressed in the finest gowns and suits money could buy. The screech of chair legs against stone, hand shaking, "how do you do's" and "good evenings" broke out and in the commotion, Gillian appeared at my side.

"Come, let us stroll out to the front entrance and get some fresh air"

*

My sire led me from the hall and out of the front doors through the lobby, where we were greeted by a pleasantly warm breeze. Gillian closed both doors behind us and joined me at the bottom of the stone steps.

"Here, have a cigar."

He produced two cubans from his inner pocket and lit them both with a match, then we stood in silence for a little while, just smoking.

"I want you to practise utilising your supernatural senses with Carmen, and learn to separate and combine the senses so that you may use them to your advantage."

He said, upon a sudden, looking down at me with a most peculiar expression.

"I want you to know ... I have complete and utter confidence in you."

His faith showed with sincerity upon his ancient, but no less youthful face. My own mind was dominated by worries that needed his guidance to assuage.

"That will be enough instruction from me for tonight ... finish your cigar and find me indoors, we have much still to prepare."

With that he ceased his smoking, put his cigar out on the nearest stone step then stowed away what was left in his pocket. No sooner than he had reached the doorway, I called out his name.

"Gillian wait, I have something on my mind I must share with you."

He halted, clasping his hands behind his back and adopting a look of mild interest.

"I have noticed you seem to be more distant than is usual, I merely wished to give you the freedom to confide in me when you saw fit to do so."

"There is a young lady who lives across the river, beset from all angles by poverty and misery. I have been visiting her and I confess ... I have a growing fire within my heart for this woman. I fear that, through no intentional actions I assure you, I may have put her life in danger along with the lives of those she loves."

I explained and in that same instant, I felt as if a great weight had been lifted from my shoulders. My sire considered this for several minutes before eventually giving a reply.

"I have known for some time that you feel your immortal life is akin to being adrift at sea, with no particular direction or purpose. I feel this woman you speak of - "

" - Maria - "

" - has given you a sense of purpose, but Carlos, I must insist you focus your attention on bringing an end to Raoul. That is the only way you can protect her. Imagine what would become of this woman if we allow Raoul to drive us out and take control of Sevilla?"

He left the question hanging in the air; soon enough, gruesome images manifested themselves and I shuddered, chasing them away. I could not tell with any certainty whether Gillian cared more for my plight or his own, but I was unwilling to start a dispute with him so I said nothing of my doubts.

"I thank you for your wisdom, it truly knows no bounds." I said with a smile.

Gillian gave a curt nod and headed inside; his silhouette sliced shadows through the lamp light that spilled onto the forecourt, then their bright luminescence drowned completely when he pulled shut the door behind him.

Chapter Seven

I stood by the window in my room peeping through a set of heavy, royal blue curtains, angled just right so that the sun sparkling off the surface of the guadalquivir couldn't burn my skin.

I had been restlessly pacing most of the day whilst Gillian secluded himself in his office, finalising the plans for this evening. Wracked with agitation I found myself smoking cigar after cigar, alongside many a glass of whisky.

I sat in my wingback chair mulling things over then after a while, then began to pursue my copy of Great Expectations.

Maria played constantly on my thoughts and there apparently was nothing I could do to banish my worries.

If I returned to see her it would cause us both more harm than good; I ruminated on this for a while and had many aggressive changes of heart, until I could stand the pacing no longer. At that decisive moment, Carmen stepped into the room without so much as a knock and shut the door.

We stared without speaking to each other, then her eyes shifted to something behind me.

"That carnation is beautiful, Señor."

She said, her sweet voice like honey dripping from a comb.

The vampire witch oozed elegance; she almost glided across the room to stand before me. She wore a baby blue gown over white skirts, her caramel hair was pinned up in elaborate ringlets and topped with a matching, dainty little hat.

It was secured to her head with pink ribbons tied in a bow under her chin. I cleared my throat, realising I had not responded to her comment.

"Gracias, Señorita. It was a gift from..."

I let the words trail off into nothing, realising that I had no idea what Maria and I were to each other.

" ... a friend."

I concluded, finally. Carmen gave me a lovely yet all too understanding smile.

"You are bewitched by a charming young lady are you not, Senor Fernandez?"

She deduced, moving to stand by the marble mantle piece atop which sat the lovely red flower in a clear, empty wine bottle with some water. I hadn't any good reason not to be open with Carmen; to attempt it would be to insult her intelligence.

"Yes, Señorita, it is so."

One of her blonde eyebrows rose a fraction; I could only surmise that she felt my candour to be refreshing, in a world where men hide their true feelings and women were discouraged from asking the latter such bold questions.

Her brown eyes bore into mine with an unspoken challenge, not unlike the way Gillian's did when he was confounded by new ideas. Perhaps it was this which drew my sire to her so effortlessly.

"I was a young lady, once."

Carmen announced, as if continuing a previous conversation on the matter.

"I was the object of many a man's dreams and desires ... that is until they realised I was a witch and opted to have me burned at the stake."

She turned away from the mantelpiece and wandered across to the curtains, peeping out as I had from the sides.

"Gillian saved me."

She continued.

"He later told me he couldn't allow humanity to destroy such a rare and beautiful jewel and that he almost reawakened his own magic in his anger, something he had blocked for hundreds of years. Such an act could've resulted in a grave explosion of dangerous magic, so I cast a light sleeping spell over the assembly to avoid a massacre. Afterwards, he took me to his ship waiting on the coast of the Cote d'Azur, from there we sailed to his home land of Greece."

Her words permeated the space around us and Carmen let them sit, then turned to face me again. I once again took my seat in the armchair; I couldn't help thinking how much happier my sire would be if he and Carmen were to settle down, but I said nothing of this.

Instead, I chose another line of questioning. I recalled a time when I was newly turned and Gillian revealed to me a little of his past in a particular conversation. Before he turned into a vampire five thousand years ago, Gillian had already been blessed with the gift of magic.

His paternal family were part of a long line of powerful witch doctors, or shamans, a skill that naturally passed down to my sire. I knew nothing of his experience in this, only that some couple of hundred years later something caused Gillian to suppress that side of himself. From then on he was for all intents and purposes no longer a hybrid, but simply just a vampire.

"Forgive me for prying but, I was wondering if you know the details of how Gillian came to give up the practice of shamanism? It's just that ... he has never spoken of it with me. I only discovered that he was a hybrid a couple of years into our knowing each other."

Carmen's smile evaporated, and sadness crossed her features for the briefest time.

"Alas, I must regretfully admit that even I know this story not. He has never told me a thing, though I'm almost certain it had to do with his own sire, Ava"

She admitted, back to admiring Maria's carnation.

"I think, Senor Fernandez, that you will have a little more luck with this young lady of yours. I say, if she means so much to you then why not keep her by your side forever? Such a gesture would surely keep her from harm and would it not transcend all other gifts you could bestow?"

Her suggestion was a stroke of brilliance I hadn't yet considered. Maria certainly had a curious and open mind, which would be invaluable to her in such a life.

She dreamed of escaping her miserable situation - a sound goal for which to strive - but what of her younger siblings, whom I had heard softly sleeping in their beds last I visited? Surely she would not want to leave them?

Carmen had noticed the cogs in my mind turning and offered her help once again.

"All you can do is make the offer, only then will you know truly if it is meant to last."

She smiled, then closed her eyes and cupped the carnation in her hands. Enthralled, I watched her mutter an incantation which set the flower aglow. Light shone through her fingers, then died away.

"This gift is immortal now, it will never stop blooming and its beauty will never fade. Now she is with you, whatever happens."

I had no idea what to say to such a kindness. I stuttered over my words until coherent speech was again possible.

"Muchas gracias señorita, no one has ever been so thoughtful."

Once she had left, I wrestled my disorganised mind into order and quickly came up with a plan. I would sneak away at sunset and come clean about what I truly was; I would have to be precise if my absence was to go unnoticed, however the idea that she may reject me was far more worrisome.

Chapter Eight

When I arrived at Maria's home she was sleeping soundly in her bed; I felt awful about waking her but alas, there really wasn't much choice in the matter.

I stepped onto the balcony and with a gentle hand, tapped my knuckled lightly against the shutters. Her eyelids fluttered and she lifted herself out of bed to see who had disturbed her dreams.

"Carlos, is that you?"

She mumbled, using the back of her hand to rub her gluey eyes open. She appeared surprised, but pleasantly so.

"I cannot fathom why you insist on ... keeping such late hours."

Maria attempted to stifle a yawn as she spoke, but in vain.

"If my father catches you here, he will become quite unreasonable."

"I do not care for your father, I came to see you. I have ... "

Sadly, I realised I hadn't the slightest clue how to present my offer. The young lady did not even know vampires existed, let alone that I was one of them.

It seemed to me I had no choice but to do that which Gillian had always sought to avoid; throwing caution to the winds was my last chance.

"I trust you remember our first conversation, in which you expressed a desire to travel and to see more of the world?" I began.

"Of course I remember."

"Have you ever wondered if, perhaps, there's much more to this life than meets the eye? What I mean to say is that, the world hides many more secrets than you could ever have imagined."

She looked at me with some concern and a little intrigue. One of her eyebrows arched upwards, spelling out her puzzlement.

"Are you about to tell me the reasoning behind your always visiting so late?"

She deduced, leaning her elbows on the balcony.

"I'm here to offer you a new life, Señorita. One filled with boundless opportunity. Be that as it may, I would be remiss if I did not inform you of the finer details. Such an undertaking would require you to ... change. To become like me."

She leaned forward until the heat of her pumping blood was physically tangible; her eyes were shining brown moons and I the sea tide, pulled mercilessly in by her gravity.

"What *are* you, Carlos?"

She asked. I hesitated for only a fraction of a second.

"I'm a vampire."

I had pictured this moment before it came. In those imaginings Maria saw me as a demon, she fled from me and locked all windows and doors, beseeching me never to return.

"A vampire?" She repeated "well that explains a lot."

I allowed her to think in silence, though every part of me was desperately screaming for an answer.

"So ... you drink the blood of the living to survive?"

"Yes, but only from those who are willing. If they are not, I am able to repair wounds with my blood and erase memories with hypnosis. I can teach you the ways taught to me by my sire, you wouldn't have to kill anybody."

I secretly, selfishly hoped this point might sway her in my favour. She chewed her lip absently and a warm breeze swirled the curtains behind her into a frenzy.

"What about my brothers and sisters, I cannot simply leave them behind ... who will protect them?"

"Your absence can only serve to make them stronger, as I'm sure my absence did when I left my father. I did not leave willingly; he had seized an opportunity to save me from dying of a terrible disease and begged me to take it. He knew it was unlikely that we'd ever meet again ... your siblings will grow hoping you have found happiness and I can make you beyond happy, so they will not hope in vain."

I reached out and took Maria's hand in mine, cradling her dark skinned face in my other.

Initially she flinched at the icy coldness of my touch, but then she relaxed with a contented sigh. I couldn't take my eyes away from her soft, pink mouth. I longed to feel her against my flesh and I could hide it no longer.

I leaned in until our lips met with an explosion of unbridled passion. Maria made a noise in her throat; her surprise at my sudden advance quickly morphed into arousal.

She allowed my hands to roam over the skin of her neck and shoulders, as she wound her own fingers into my tousled brown hair, pulling me closer.

When the kiss ended her heart was hammering like the beating wings of a hummingbird. My own stayed as silent and still as ever; I had no doubt that if I were still human, it too would be wildly accelerating.

"Oh my..."

She breathed deeply which caused her bosom to heave. Her alluring lashes fluttered and her eyes had in them a glassy sparkle.

"I'll do it, I'll follow you into this madness. The Lord must've heard my prayers - and I say this with no offence intended - I have never heard of a prayer being answered in so heathen a manner."

I have to admit, it was difficult not to grin from ear to ear so gaily that I was in danger of looking mad.

"Thank you."

I whispered, and joy washed over me, wave after glorious wave. The last vestiges of blue in the sky had been replaced by dark navy, dotted intermittently with sparkling white stars.

Gillian would grow irritable if I stayed out any longer; before I could reasonably leave, I had a duty to tell Maria what was about to happen tonight. She'd been watching me silently as I went through the thought process.

I snatched her hands and held them close to my chest, which drew her closer and wafted her intoxicating smell over me.

"I have one more thing to tell you, sweet Maria, I think it is best done whilst I am in the throes of candour."

I told her.

"Pray tell, Carlos, what must you reveal to me now?"

"I confess, there is an imminent danger in this town that needs to be dealt with. I shall return to come and get you when it is safe ... will you wait for me?"

Her smile was not prejudiced, but full of understanding.

"Of course, I will happily wait for your return. I can pack a small bag with what little I have in the meantime ... though I can't help but wonder how much use garden pruning shears will be in the next life."

I couldn't help a chuckle; my heart soared for the second time that evening as I marvelled at her being.

"They will be of use to you as a vampire, if that is what you choose. Goodnight Senorita, I will return."

I promised, planting one last kiss on her warm hand. Picturing Gillian's huffing and chuntering in my mind's eye, I knew I could delay leaving no further. I dropped fifty feet from the balcony and landed on the cobbled street, bending my knees to absorb the shock of impact.

At that moment, I knew it. I knew beyond any doubt that I was the happiest vampire in Sevilla.

Chapter Nine

Gillian locked his restless, conspiratorial eyes on me; the others had gone ahead of us, now he placed a strong hand on my shoulder and squeezed.

"Ensure your senses are sharp tonight, my friend, don't let your guard down. And *do* try not to get yourself killed, I've grown rather fond of you if you'll believe it."

I smiled earnestly.

"I do believe it, and I can honestly say I feel the same way." I admitted "Good luck, and Godspeed."

My sire tipped his hat, then he left the same way as our brethren. Carmen was the only straggler left; she emerged from the building with bright, yellow light spilling out behind her through the open doors.

We exchanged a glance and nods of encouragement, then took after the retinue of vampires defending Sevilla against The Red Wolf.

*

Eerie quiet stole through the streets alongside our army of undead, and each small or insignificant noise became sinister in the collective, preemptive thoughts of impending violence. Gillian strode next to me and Carmen flanked my other side, the three of us were enveloped by our comrades as the infamous bell tower loomed into view.

The city was illuminated by the occasional gas powered street lamps, but even as the light of their fires skittered across the still river, so too did they emphasise patches of darkness and wreak havoc on my imagination.

"There they are."

I pointed out the deserted square ahead which preceded the bell tower; off to the right side stood an alley, wherein blacked out silhouettes of roughly a dozen vampires crouched, lying in wait.

"Stop."

Gillian halted the procession of our clan with a single gesture. Snarling reached our ears, then bodies started to emerge. Pale faces descended the sides of buildings, crawled from sewers or balconies and materialised from the shadows of arches and doorways.

It was clear we were surrounded; I looked back to confirm our enemy had indeed circled around us.

"But where is their ring leader, and his two sycophants?"

Gillian wondered. There wasn't time enough for answers, as the newly turned vampires screeched out a battle cry and leapt in unison for their first attack.

Marcelo reacted with ferociously good timing; he whipped out a clawed hand and caught the nearest assailant by the neck. Carmen's graceful beauty vanished instantly; it was possible she looked scarier now than Gillian ever had.

Jinfeng was faster than a speeding bullet; I dived out of her path when she lunged at a rival vampire and disembowelled the poor creature before my very eyes. Had I neglected to move I'm certain she would've cleaved through me, blinded as she was by bloodlust.

Gillian disappeared into the foray; I accosted three young vampires whose faces regretfully matched the illustrations of missing locals from the newspaper.

I twisted their necks for good measure and moved on, then a fist barreled into my cheek and I hit the ground hard. Congealed, dark blood pooled in my mouth. I spat on the floor and looked about for my challenger, only to find Gillian standing there.

"Carlos!"

"Gillian."

"They're nowhere to be seen."

I said simply.

"I know."

Gillian offered a hand to pull me up.

"Take the rooftops over yonder and see what you can hear, I'll climb the bell tower for a better vantage point."

I nodded in agreement and we separated for our destinations. I sped to the nearest house, clambered up on the portico and onto the roof; with closed eyes, I drowned out the cacophony of noises and inhaled a deep lungful of air. It was all nonsense at first, until I calmed my nerves and focused my mind.

I picked up Raoul's scent close by, but it was tangled with another, foreign aroma. It was of a wood that wasn't native to this place, and its potency suggested it had been recently carved and layered with resin or wax.

I kept my eyes closed against the warm breeze and focused on the direction of the bell tower, towards which Gillian was headed as he fought through a slew of young vampires. The voices of my enemies echoed in my ears, alongside the unmistakable *swooshing* of a sword.

" ... We cannot afford any mistakes tonight."

Raoul was saying.

A pair of boots clacked in a pacing, back and forth rhythm over the floor of the bell tower's highest platform, which was usually only frequented by maintenance and cleaning crews. Another was with him; I ceased breathing and strained to maximise my hearing.

" ... What is it you require of us?"

Jameson asked; his oily, purring voice was instantly recognisable. Incredibly, I was able to hear Raoul run a finger along the length of his wooden blade. The thought of a weapon capable of permanently ending a vampire, sent an icy shiver down my spine, and lifted the fine hairs on my neck.

"...You may be of great use to me, if you can do but one thing."

"What is it, Senor?"

"That child who follows the old man around, what's his name?"

Raoul asked. His tone was inquisitive, but alas, there was no doubting the callousness which lay beneath his words.

"Carlos Fernandez."

Jameson offered.

"Yes, that one. He'll provide too great a distraction and we cannot allow him to aid his sire. What I'd very much like you to do, is take Peter and make certain that little runt is occupied. If I'm to ambush Gillian, I'll need all the advantage I can get."

"Of course, Señor." Jameson agreed. "I believe I know exactly the thing."

"Good. This ebony sword is completely unique, you know. There's nothing of its likeness in the entire world, but even that will not…"

I allowed Raoul's words to trail off into nothingness. He didn't intend to win honourably or accept fealty from my sire, at all. He wanted Gillian dead. If my heart could still beat, at that moment it would've faltered.

'I believe I know just the thing.'

Jameson had said. Cold realisation hit me; I needed to warn Gillian, but no sooner than I'd decided to protect my sire did another thought stopped me.

What did Jameson know would prevent me from coming to Gillian's aid?

"Maria."

I muttered. Her name was the key that unlocked my limbs and allowed me to move.

I flew like an arrow over the rooftops, praying to a God I had already forsaken, that I wouldn't be too late.

Chapter Ten

I never realised the full extent of my speed, until I was in danger of losing everything. The world blurred around me as I raced to save her, and I didn't stop until I landed on her balcony.

When I smelled blood from within the building, any hope I'd had was dashed against the floor and shattered into a thousand pieces. Her doors were wide open and out of them billowed the sheer white curtains.

Any further delusions of hope were crushed into shards when I was able to walk into her room unhindered; vampires may only enter a human dwelling without verbal invitation, if the owner dies and no deeds have been signed over.

Maria's father lay sprawled up the staircase, he had vicious slashes to his midriff and his innards spilled like grotesque spaghetti over the floor.

Two young children lay motionless in a dark corner of the landing, tossed aside and discarded like candy wrappers. I couldn't even bear to look.

Then there was her. The bastards had arranged her body to look as if she could've been sleeping; her hands were crossed over her chest and placed beneath them was a single, white carnation.

I fell to my knees at the sight of her aggressive neck wound, I felt hollow, staring into her brown eyes which were fixed on the ceiling, unmoving.

The blood staining her and the bedclothes was sticky and warm - to think I could've saved her had I arrived a second earlier. It was torture. It was my fault alone that this young woman would never see the light of another day.

If I had only let her be; if not for my own selfish need to return, she could have lived. I must've crouched at her bedside for an eternity thinking of the life I had been about to give her, the freedom she would never experience.

Finally, I managed to force myself up from the floor. I rummaged in my pocket and found two silver pennies.

I delicately closed Maria's eyes, then placed a coin on each. I pressed my lips gently against hers one more time; we were the same temperature now, though it saddened me greatly not to feel the warmth she had always emanated.

There was nothing else I could do, so I turned away from the scene of destruction to leave, overwhelmed by waves of grief and desire for vengeance. A glimmer of white on the bedside table caught my eye, and I turned back.

There, next to a single burning candlestick in a brass holder, was a note. I picked it up with contempt, instantly recognising the infamous wolf's head drawn in her blood. Underneath, the message read:

You should learn to take better care of your pets, amigo.

James & Peter

I crumpled the note in my fist with burning hatred coursing through my veins, scorching a hole in my heart. There was nothing more I could do for Maria now, except perhaps one thing.

I was almost airborne as I flitted across town, jumping along the terracotta brick buildings and back down the length of the Guadalquivir.

Soon, I had the bell tower in my sights. I could hear everything; at the docks vampires were being ripped apart, but I couldn't be sure which clan had the advantage over whom.

It was none of my concern, my focus remained on the bell tower. I could hear Raoul's sword slashing through the air and Gillian dancing about the space to avoid it, goading him.

One wrong move saw him gasp in pain and fall; Raoul had finally landed a deadly blow.

A feral snarl escaped my lips in a blind rage. I launched myself against the tower wall, leaving tiny finger tip shaped craters in the stone as I climbed. I hauled myself easily over the top edge and landed, crouched like a starving tiger.

Raoul hissed, spinning around to face me. Gillian was slumped in the corner holding an arm across his chest, where blood spilled out from the wood inflicted injury. My sire grinned from ear to ear when his eyes locked with mine, showing off his dazzling pearly whites.

"I knew I could count on you, my brother."

He said. The weakness in his voice couldn't hide the pride that swelled in his chest. Raoul snarled with a face like a wrinkled, angry boulder; he was the only one I had eyes for.

"You fool."

I spat, my jaws clenched tightly together. Raoul laughed, though he continued to back away as I advanced.

"I see Jameson and that fat oaf have just been demoted ... where have you left their bodies?"

"I missed them this time ... when I do find them I'll be sure to send their corpses to your doorstep. Perhaps I'll mail them in pieces, just as they did with the life of a woman I cared for."

We continued to circle the huge brass bell in the centre of the square platform; Raoul grew ever more agitated by the minute. Gillian had now joined me, bolstering my resolve to finish the deed that had to be done.

"None of that matters, for I shall be the one who leaves pieces of you scattered all over the neighbourhood!"

The Red Wolf let out a mad, desperate cackle of a laugh; his scarred face lit up as a half moon slid out from behind a cloud. I lowered into a crouch and a deep growl rumbled through my fangs.

Raoul pounced with his teeth bared and latched onto my throat, sending shock waves reverberating through me. Gillian appeared behind him when I toppled and hit my head on the sharp stone edge of the bell tower's platform.

The painful throbbing ebbed away as the wound closed; Gillian yanked The Red Wolf by the scruff of his trench coat and forcibly took his sword. I took hold of his collar and swung him over the edge of the tower, so I was the only thing preventing his fall into the void.

Gillian hurled the sword through the air and I reached out and caught it; I held its deadly point directly over Raoul's heart. Leaning close, I whispered in his ear.

"When I find Jameson and Peter, I will reign down on them like a swarm of locusts, and make them regret this night. As for you ... I will allow your sword to teach you what a real bite feels like."

With that I thrust the sword forward and plunging it deep into The Red Wolf's heart. It emerged out the other side of his back soaked in dark, congealed blood.

His screams pierced the night; I released his collar and let him fall.

Chapter Eleven

When I first became a vampire, I had no idea what my purpose was.

I travelled Europe with my sire, who taught me not only the most efficient way of procuring blood from humans, but also how to maintain my respect for them. He taught me to fight my battles with honour, how to single out heartbeats and facial features in complete darkness.

Yet despite the countless bottles of whiskey shared and packs of cigars smoked, I always felt I had no place amongst the undead.

As I arranged flowers around Maria's still form on the wooden raft, I knew beyond any doubt I had found that purpose. There was no moon to see that night, only a sky full of stars and quietly lapping waves.

Gillian stood on one side of me; he wore a black silk tuxedo with a matching top hat. His breast pocket was adorned with a white rose, he stood proud and sure with his hands clasped behind him. Carmen stood on my other side, wearing a delicate chiffon veil and a black lace dress.

I'd chosen to send Maria off by the sea, on a quiet stretch of beach far from the busy docks of Sevilla. I knew she would've appreciated the symbolic gesture, yet now the moment of parting had come, I was numb. I could not take my eyes away from her white dress; it was the perfect representation of her pureness and vitality.

I thought of Jameson and his lackey, the soulless demons who'd snatched both away from her. The thought of it rekindled my fury and grief.

I had all but forgotten my surroundings, until Gillian placed a gentle hand on my shoulder, bringing me back.

"Are you going to say something for her, my friend?"

He asked. At the same time Carmen took my hand, and laced her fingers with mine.

"Yes, I ...."

Shaking myself internally, I gathered together my thoughts, keeping my eyes on the sparkling horizon.

"For a short while, you were the light in my life. Visiting you each evening gave me a purpose which was something I had ... hadn't had in years."

I stopped, fearing my voice would break; I leaned forward and tucked a strand of curly black hair behind Maria's ear.

"I would have shown you everything there is to see, we could have done all there is to do. I would have married you, eventually, and I could've taken you away from all that pain and sorrow ... I could've made you invincible, like me. As I cannot do that, I instead will make it my purpose to find the two responsible for visiting this monstrosity upon you. I will see to it that justice is served, this I swear."

There were no more words, nothing more would come. I extracted a box of matches from my breast pocket and struck one, throwing it onto the pyre. The sweet perfume from her carnations rose high into the air as the flames spread, masking the smell of burning flesh.

Together, we three pushed the pyre into the water and watched as deep orange flames shone against the darkness of the night, in the same way Maria had eradicated my own darkness.

She bobbed away across the waves and I stayed there, looking out to sea long after her silhouette had disappeared, and both Carmen and Gillian were gone.

All I had left was time, time to ruminate on the promise I'd made to us both. I cared not whether it would take one century or five, but before my life's end I would make Jameson and Peter pay for this moment.

I would never forget and I would never rest. I would hunt them down and kill them both, even if it was the last thing I would ever do.

Part Two: Ailana

160 Years Later

Chapter Twelve

The fire came in flashes of images afterwards, but they were imprinted on my memory indefinitely.

One thing was salvaged from the house, apart from me; a silver chain which held a photo locket pendant, inside were two little pictures of my mum and dad. It was all my fault; I kept thinking it over and over, as I sat dazed at my neighbors dining room table, while plumes of black smoke and angry, amber flames continued to devour my childhood home.

I didn't speak a word until auntie Helena came to pick me up; when she clacked over the threshold in her shiny black high heels, I ran to her in a stream of blubbering and tears.

She thanked the neighbors for watching over me and I fell asleep in the car on the way to her house in Whitby, so it wasn't until the next day that I could explain to my family what had really happened.

Everyone was sympathetic, at first. As the years went by their sympathy waned, along with my magical gifts - a talent my whole family shared.

The coven served as nothing but a reminder of my past mistakes, and I was nothing to them but a painful reminder that my parents were no longer with us.

Chapter Thirteen

When I got the phone call from my aunt that day, a shudder slithered down my spine with a sharp chill.

Of course.

I thought at the time.

I haven't heard from you since I left, now you're going to give me stick about not practising at home.

I ignored the repetitive, buzzing chimes with a small pang of guilt and carried on leafing through brainstorming sheets and collages for my coursework project. But the phone kept ringing, until eventually I threw in the towel and decided to see what all the fuss was about.

There was nothing on the other line at first except the fragmented scuffling of static, then the rich smooth voice of my aunt Helena.

"Ailana, it's me, Helena."

"I know it's you, your number's saved in my phone. What's up, I'm kinda in the middle of coursework here."

I took a sip from my can of beer as I spoke, trying to ignore the guilt I felt for using my school work as a means to excuse me from any lectures about not practising magic.

"Nanny Eileen has just been on the phone," Helena announced "Grampa Maurice is dead."

"Oh."

Shit.

The meaning of her words sunk slowly into my brain, like a sloth climbing to the top of a very large tree. I suddenly felt their impact for real, and broke the silence that had stretched between us over the phone line.

"What happened?"

"Vampire attack. Nanny Eileen woke and was able to fend off the creature, but by then it was too late."

"I'm so sorry…auntie. Have the rest of the family been told?"

"Of course. We need you to come down to Wiltshire to complete the Lectio Ritu, Ailana."

It never ceased to amaze me how quickly my aunt could brush off a disaster or mishap, and click into management mode.

"But I left the coven, I *told* you I don't want to practise anymore."

I got up from the bed and paced back and forth. It was so cramped; belongings and garbage were chucked pel-mel over the floor and disarray was everywhere, but I was used to it. In fact, I bet I could navigate the piles of trash without so much as a wobble backwards in my sleep.

I found myself absently staring at an old photograph on the wall; me with my best friends, Poppy and Violet. My dark curly hair was short, tied in pigtails with pink bows, and an innocent gap toothed smile underlined slanted green eyes filled with the excitement only a child can possess.

Those eyes were filled with happiness, frozen in time; That poor girl was completely unaware of the tragedy soon to befall her.

"Ailana listen to me girl, you might have turned your back on magic but it hasn't turned it's back on you. Every witch in my father's lineage needs to be there for the ritual or a new leader can't be picked, you know how this works. You're going to pack a bag and get in the car, I'll see you at nanny's house tonight at seven o'clock do you understand? I don't want to hear any excuses, I just need you to promise me you're going to be there."

I didn't reply straight away. Though my heart was aching for my grandpa, another worrisome thought was simmering away in my mind.

What if I'm chosen?

I told myself it was a ridiculous thought, there was no way I'd be chosen to run the coven after I turned my back on them.

"Ailana, are you still there?"

"Yes I'm here, I'm...I'll be there don't worry. I'll see you soon, auntie."

With that I hung up the phone. I wandered over to the window fiddling with my silver locket, a habit I'd had ever since childhood that manifested itself whenever I was filled with anxiety. The clouds above had turned a severe, steel grey. They glowered down at me as the first droplets of rain poured from the sky; the weather reflected the change in my world perfectly.

I chewed my lip while staring vaguely at my reflection in the window. My brown, springy curls were tied up in a messy bun. Green eyes like my fathers, but the shape of my mothers, were wracked with worry. I had on my favourite red and black checked lumberjack shirt with a simple black cami top; comfort first, as always.

Eventually I came to my senses and grabbed my mobile again. I texted Violet and told her that, unfortunately, I wouldn't be able to make the group project meeting this weekend, which she said was fine because she would email me whatever they were working on for my approval.

I then went about packing a small duffel bag and grabbed my keys before heading out to my car; a gift from my auntie when I turned eighteen.

Inside it was a complete mess; empty takeaway boxes, drinks cans and all sorts littered the back seats and floors, but the clutter was familiar and so went a little way towards calming my nerves.

Once I was strapped in and gazing out of the windshield, all my worries returned.

What if I get picked?

I thought again.

Don't be ridiculous, your grandpa isn't going to choose a quitter as the new leader.

I inserted the keys and the engine purred to life. I backed out of the drive and took off, more than well aware I was heading into uncharted territory and there was nothing I could do about it.

Chapter Fourteen

It was five o'clock when I finally stepped out into the warm, country air. Pink and orange clouds chased each other to the west, while dark blue hues diluted the sky left behind.

A little breeze moved between me and a small woman standing in the open front door as I pulled up. She watched me with her arms crossed against her tiny body. If I wasn't mistaken I could see a scowl beneath her large, round glasses.

She wore an elegant black cocktail dress, but had neglected to swap out her cosy slippers for proper shoes and her shoulders were only covered by a short sleeved cardigan.

Her home was surrounded by an acre of sprawling, private land and was originally built in the 1600's by our Tudor ancestors; this house had been passed down each generation of our coven ever since. Cone shaped bushes flanked the entrance and either side of the gravel path, were two immaculate green lawns covered in artfully arranged rose bushes.

Their colours varied from the deepest reds and warmest pinks, to pale yellows and even hybridised royal blues. The cottage itself lorded over the landscape surrounding it with a much subtler beauty; walls of cream and white were decorated with lace curtains drawn back in each window.

My poor Nan...

I thought, turning my engine off and taking the keys out. I tried to still my shaking hands as I grabbed my overnight bag and headed towards her. The whiff of a distant farm's manure patch travelled on the light breeze, which stole through my hair as I walked down the stone path.

I swallowed a hard knot in my throat as Nanny Eileen's stern, lined face grew closer.

"You're here too early, Ailana. I told Helena to let you all know that the ritual would commence at the earliest half six!"

She scoffed, as soon as I was within hugging distance. I leaned forward to embrace her frail body between my arms, which sent a well worn pang of guilt through my heart. From now on, I would make more of an effort to visit her, even if it meant being chastised about my magical gifts...or lack thereof.

"I thought I could come and help you out with the preparations."

I explained. Her own embrace was brief; she kept one hand on the door frame and the other loosely round my shoulders.

She was itching to talk to me about the last time we saw each other, I just knew it. That would also be the last time I saw my Grandpa alive.

I prayed she would wait until I'd brought some bottles of alcohol out from the garage, though I doubted it.

"Such a shame you had to leave the coven when you did, Ailana."

Nanny said eventually, after a moment of awkward silence.

"I know, Nan."

"Yes well, it's by the by now, but you have missed out on some wondrous years with Maurice. Did I tell you about last summer when we went to Hawaii? We stayed in that hotel near where your mother used to live...it was beautiful."

"Yes, you told me a few times on the phone." I replied stonily.

My fingers subconsciously took up their shaky fiddling with the silver locket around my neck. She knew my parents were a sore subject, but I figured she had a right to be sore about everything given what she was going through, so I said nothing.

"If you really insist on helping out, you can take yourself off to the kitchen. I've started sorting the herbs for the pyre into different piles, you can make sure they are all labelled and the correct weights have been measured for each of them."

Nan instructed me, waving her hand dismissively before turning to hobble back inside.

The interior of the cottage was like something out of a postcard; repulsive lace doilies hung on every available surface, whilst bunches of dried lavender and chamomile sat in dusty vases on almost every window sill.

The floors were covered from wall to wall with rugs of different ages and sizes; I'd forgotten that bumpy feeling under foot when walking over them, so many years had passed since I'd been here but the more I saw, the more I remembered.

The dining room was a relic of times when a younger Eileen and Maurice had sat together with

Helena and Marcus as children, playing board games and eating dinner as a family. Now, the blue rhys chairs were faded by time and the windows powdered in cobwebs.

I eventually resigned myself to organising an assortment of ingredients; we were supposed to dress the body with them so their energy mingled with my Grandpa's flesh as he burned, which would in turn enabled his spirit to come forth when we called for it. I knew the basics of everything I had to do, but a huge part of me was cringing away from the task; it made the whole afternoon a drag.

Afterwards, nanny Eileen got me to do the washing up and the hoovering, then she made me stand on a stool and attach frilly black banners to the ceilings in every room. I burned sage and palo-santo in the entrance to clear out the energy, just in time for my aunt and my cousin to arrive.

My nerves, which I'd been able to hold at bay in the wake of being so busy, now came flooding back causing a sharp, piercing sensation in my heart. Aunt Helena's sleek, grey saloon car pulled into the gravel driveway and my cousin's shining red stallion pulled in after her.

The sky had darkened whilst we'd been preparing; a dozen or so tiny silhouettes of bats could be seen darting about in the twilight, the air had lost its inviting warmth and replaced it with a chill, forcing nanny and I to don our jackets as we came out to greet the girls.

"Kitty!"

I sang, throwing my arms out to receive my ginger haired beauty of a cousin as she stepped gracefully out of the driver's seat.

"Ailana, I wasn't sure if you were coming or not sweetie."

"How could I refuse with this lot on my case?"

I joked; for the first time that day, I was genuinely happy.

Kitty squeezed me so hard I felt my bones crack in their sockets, then she let go and cupped my face with her hands, staring hard into my eyes.

Hers were bright blue and wide, her shapely figure was accentuated in a smart black jacket cinched in at the waist, a pair of black jeans, red heels and a white blouse top underneath.

The way her fiery locks twisted over and again in perfect ringlets always reminded me of Kate Winslet in Sense and Sensibility; she was a sight for sore eyes.

We squeezed each other's hands, then she went to greet nan and I, my aunt.

It was an altogether different affair with her. Aunt Helena was the spitting image of my cousin, only twenty years older. The subtle lines on her face were harsh yet somehow slender, her blue eyes were not as bright as Kitty's but they shone with a ray of intelligence that I'd always found slightly intimidating; like her mother's they conveyed a sense of haughtiness.

Her hug wasn't exactly warm, but strong and as brief as they come.

"Hello dear, I trust your journey wasn't too much of a hassle?"

"It was fine actually, I bazzed it down in about three hours. I've been helping nanny with the decorations."

Aunt Helena's smile was characteristically tight, but it warmed up significantly when she turned to her mother.

"Mummy! I'm *so* sorry..."

"Don't you worry my dear, we will get through this as a family. I've got everything ready in the house, Maurice is already dressed in his robes and waiting on the pyre. Ailana's been sorting the herbs so hopefully we won't have any mishaps."

Nan's words punched a hole through my side, as did the raised eyebrow she cast my way as she and my aunt turned to stare at me. I didn't let the pain show, I simply smiled.

"I know what-herbs-are-what, nan, relax. I've picked out aconite for his transition into the spirit world, bay laurel for communicating with his spirit and elder to bless the funeral pyre."

No-one said a word; I got the feeling they were impressed but none of them dared say so. Only Kitty noticed I wasn't happy; she smiled apologetically on their behalf, but we both knew it wasn't going to mend anything.

*

"Aren't we still waiting for Uncle Marcus?" Kitty chirped.

She was leaning against the mahogany table in nan's kitchen, with its wooden beams that ran overhead and the old, uneven tile flooring.

We'd moved grandpa straight out to the pyre, then we took ourselves off to get dressed into our ritual wear. For the women, simple black dresses that fell down to our toes, with woven brown belts at the waist. The men would both be wearing black collared shirts and trousers, though grandpa was wearing traditional embroidered robes over his.

"I shouldn't think he'll be too much longer."

I said quietly. We'd been waiting in the kitchen in silence, for the most part, which I honestly preferred.

"Mum, have you seen what's on social media right now?" Kitty said.

Helena looked up from her own phone to look at her daughter.

"What is it dear?"

"Tia from the Brownland Coven has been posting pictures of herself with her new boyfriend, who's a vampire."

Aunt Helena gasped like this was the juiciest piece of gossip she'd heard all year, though in her way still managed to sound sarcastic.

I rolled my eyes.

"Let's hope she doesn't end up in a ditch at the end of a row, like the last teenage witch who got involved with leeches. Do you remember? It was last year - what was her name - Kenya Zalotti? It was all over the country." Helena scoffed

"*Auntie!*" I gasped, but before anyone could say another word nanny shuffled in from outside and slammed the door.

"So,"

Nanny Eileen began; she clapped her hands together and came to stand in the middle of us, thankfully bringing an end to the awkward conversation.

"Marcus has just arrived, when he gets in we'll go out to the pyre and get started."

Marcus stomped in soon after this announcement; he was already wearing a black shirt but had left the top few buttons undone, exposing his broad chest. His bulky frame was by no means over large, but his short, prickly haircut gave the impression he was not to be messed with. Around his neck was a length of thin leather cord holding a silver Thor's hammer.

"Alright mum sorry I'm late, the traffic was unbelievable."

He said gruffly, as he kissed both of nan's cheeks in turn. He bestowed the same cordial greeting on my cousin and aunt, but gave me a quick once over and a half smile before heading into the conservatory with the others.

My hands were shaking again.

Just as long as I don't get picked, we'll be fine...

I kept telling myself, but eventually I lost the thread of all my thoughts. In no time at all we'd headed into the garden, lit the torches and stuck one in each corner of the pyre.

Grandpa Maurice looked peaceful; his lined face and grey hair glowed by the orange firelight as it danced across him. Nan had sprinkled the herbs I'd chosen over his funeral gown so they covered his body, and she herself had on a delicate, silver headband which dipped in the middle between her eyebrows and rested just above her ears. She wore this as a symbol of respect for her dead husband; it also marked that she would be substitute leader if anything went wrong with the ritual.

I snuck a glance at Kitty; her face was filled with horror as she stared at grandpa's body. I knew how close they'd been, but to her due, she held the tears at bay and stood proudly. She grasped hold of my hand and her mother's as we took our places around the pyre.

Nan held hands with Marcus and Helena and I took my uncle's other hand to complete the circle. I couldn't hide my sweaty palms, even though I'd desperately wiped them on my dress before we joined into a circle; within minutes they were slick with moisture all over again.

Helena's face was a blank mask, I couldn't tell if she was simply watching the events unfold or if the plain arrangement of her features hid a much darker pain.

"Begin the chant."

Nanny Eileen directed; her head was held high and her eyes were closed against the smoke from the flames.

"Fire for the deceased, release his spirit. May he choose his succession."

We all repeated the words in a low monotone, over and again until the flames turned white and a glowing orb rose over my grandpa.

The orb swirled and morphed into cloud, its shape was barely visible but to those of us who'd known him, the figure of our coven leader's spirit ascending over the funeral pyre was instantly recognizable.

My heart hammered madly in my chest, like a crazed inmate desperate to break free of her prison. The faces of my family were reduced to ghosts, as the bright flames washed out all colour.

They stared admirably up at the spirit of Maurice, then nan broke the circle of hands by raising her own for silence. The chanting stopped and she addressed my grandpa.

"Maurice, you have been called forth one last time by your coven to choose a successor, before crossing over into the realm of the dead to claim your eternal rest. Give us your answer, or forever more leave us in turmoil."

I looked from nanny to grandpa's spirit, waiting on tender-hooks with my heart jumping up my throat. Grandpa didn't move immediately; he lingered above us for a moment or two, faced with a silence that could be pierced with a knife.

Eventually, he sailed down on an invisible breeze, moving painfully slow. Initially it didn't seem like he had a particular direction in mind, then he started moving towards where I was standing.

He's picked Kitty, oh good for her.

I thought desperately, only he didn't stop in front of my cousin.

He stopped in front of me. A faint voice spoke next to my ear and I had a vague sense that I was the only one who could hear it.

"Ailana you must believe in yourself, you are the one who will lead this coven to greatness. In time, you will realise just how much power you carry."

At that moment, the spirit of my grandpa joined my own body; I was surrounded by his being. My stomach hurled as I was doused in coldness, then the feeling passed.

The flames of the fire went back to their usual orange and the faces of my family could be seen through the smoke; their shock and disbelief needled into me with greater ferocity every second that passed.

No one spoke, nor did they move a muscle. Kitty was the first to attempt to offer her congratulations; as soon as she took my hand and turned her understanding smile on me, a jolt went up my arm and shocked my brain into gear. Usually, a feast and the bestowing of gifts on the new leader would follow the Lectio Ritu, but I couldn't even think straight.

The moment I'd dreaded had come. I pulled my hand out of hers, which earned me a soul wrenching look of hurt, then I turned around and walked back into the house, grabbed my bag from the sofa and headed out the front door.

My whole body shook with emotion as I fished my car keys out and clicked the button to unlock my car. Kitty appeared in the doorway of the house. She clearly wanted me to come back, but I couldn't face it.

Not her sympathy, nor the rest of my family's bewildered reaction to a title I didn't even want. Choking back tears, I reversed the car out of the driveway and pulled away, tearing from the house at top speed.

Chapter Fifteen

The journey back to Cleethorpes was a nightmare. All the main roads were jammed, so instead I took the dark, winding side roads which made the car bounce up and down and around bends lined with spectral, blacked out trees.

Rain lashed at the windows and I could barely see ahead; I felt sure something was following me, but I managed to convince myself I was just being paranoid.

Even my favourite indie playlist did nothing to drown out the erratic thoughts; I was flying along at one hundred and thirty miles an hour, without realising, absorbed as I was in my own turmoil. My worst fear had come alive, I was the leader of my family's coven now. In all honesty, I felt like a fraud.

Two years ago, I left Whitby and went back to Cleethorpes to study Film and Media, hoping I'd get a break from this kinda shit. But like a cancerous speck of black mould, it was only a matter of time before it grew back and reared its ugly head.

*

The streets were empty when I arrived home. Bitter wind tangled my hair between its harsh, unforgiving fingers and I pulled my coat closer to cover my neck. Now I was alone in the open, the raised hairs on my arms screamed at me to get inside.

The feeling I was being watched was stronger than ever. Still, at least I was on familiar ground. After double checking the car was locked, I made a beeline for the front door of my flat.

I was renting an old, semi-detached house converted into two flats near the seafront.

The front door was made from dark oak, with two half length glass panels and matching windows either side, which framed identical sets of closed curtains. The original red brick archway loomed overhead, its middle piece fashioned into what I guessed was once supposed to be a gargoyle. I let myself in and hurriedly locked the front door behind me, releasing a lungful of air I hadn't realised I'd been holding.

"Jesus Christ..."

I muttered under my breath, leaning my butt against the door with my hands on my knees for support. Eerie quiet stole through the apartment and suddenly, I didn't relish the thought of being alone in my own home. Every shadow was warped in the gloom, each creaking pipe or loose floorboard made me jumpy and skittish.

I got the kettle on and decided to call Violet while I made filter coffee.

"Aila, what the fuck? It's nearly three in the *morning* mate."

She complained, her voice thick with tiredness.

"I've had a row with my family ... c'mon talk to me, y'know you want to." I begged.

I could practically hear her eyes roll; she made a noise in her throat like a lion coughing up phlegm, then the kettle finished boiling and I poured hot water into the cafetier.

"Thanks Vi, I owe ya one."

I headed to my bedroom; the house was the same bomb site it usually was, but cloaked in darkness everything threw shapes that played tricks on my mind. I scurried into my room and shut myself in.

"So come on then, what's happened?"

"It's complicated Vi, all I can say is that they're putting a lot of pressure on me lately." I told her, placing my steaming mug on the bedside table.

"What kind of pressure?"

I shrugged awkwardly.

"I don't know just...stuff to do with family tradition. I'm not really into it and they really are and it's a huge cock sucking mess."

Violet gave me a sympathetic tut.

"I'll do your nails for ya tomorrow babes, maybe that'll stop all this whinin' aye?"

I smiled to myself, at ease knowing she would never judge me. It fell quiet for a moment, then a rustle sounded from outside; when I looked to see what it was my heart stopped dead.

An unfamiliar face stared back through the window, bearing two sets of hideous fangs. I let out a blood curdling scream.

"What the hell's going on?" Violet demanded.

"It's nothing, there's a spider in my room - gotta go!"

I'd barely ended the call when the creature crashed in through my window as if fired from a cannon, leaving sparkling shards of glass littered all over the cream carpet.

The dark mass unfurled into a skinny, dirty man.

When he straightened himself up he towered over me; I quaked in silence across the room. His face was dominated by a large, beak-like nose and small, deep set blue eyes.

His hair was dirty blonde and held back in an oily ponytail, but worst of all were his teeth; coated in dry blood and a little grizzle, his four canines were sharp enough to slice through skin to the bone. I swear I nearly pissed my pants.

"How nice it was of your friend to come by with her spare key whilst you were away, and invite my comrade and I in so we could introduce ourselves."

He purred in a slippery, eel-like voice. That was when a second, much larger vampire landed on the sill. He perched there like a cat, bald headed and so large it was a question of whether he would fit through the ruined window at all.

He wore a black shirt under a pair of mud and blood spattered denim dungarees and industrial boots. They stared at me with a kind of need and hunger in their cold eyes that I shrank beneath them, almost squatting on the floor. Their glare was akin to that of a hunting lion, preparing to pounce the unfortunate gazelle.

"What...what have you done to Violet?"

I sputtered, finally finding my voice.

"We've done nothing to her, other than a little hypnotic persuasion. I am Jameson, in eternal service of The Red Wolf Gang of Europe. This is my friend and cohort, Peter. We have come to take your head so we can collect our bounty."

"I have literally *no idea* what you're talking about!"

"Of course you don't, that's the way it's supposed to be."

Without warning, the vampire flitted across the space that separated us and grabbed for me with a speed that defied normality. In a second he had an arm around my neck and the other holding my own arm out, ready to bite. The sound of my skin tearing and blood spurting was nearly enough to make my vision black out.

Don't you dare give up, not now!

I screamed in agony; after years of practice holding down my magic, the lid on the jar was secure and tight. I couldn't free it, all I had was a terrified voice in my head demanding I get out; I was as helpless as any human.

"HEY! Jameson, Peter!"

A Spaniard by the sound of him, another vampire was crouched in the window glaring at the two assailants. He was skinnier and shorter than the other two, he had a tousled head of dark hair and twinkling chocolate brown eyes.

The edges of two sharp fangs stuck out between his lips. My captor released me in surprise, hissing when he saw the third vampire who stared fixedly in my direction.

"Listen to me, Señorita, you need to invite me in. I know these two heinous vampires as I myself have hunted them for over one hundred years."

I didn't make another sound; I was frozen. All I wanted was to crumple on the floor and give in to the black out, but I couldn't. Instead, I took advantage of my attacker's momentary distraction and turned to flee the room.

I flew down the stairs and tried to wrench open the front door - realising it was locked I started to sob. I jiggled the keys left in the lock and managed to wrench it open. I stumbled out and made a break for my car.

"Senorita!"

Another scream escaped my lips as the third, unnamed vampire appeared at the passenger side window, trapping me between his body and the vehicle.

"Go away, please just leave me alone!"

I stammered. He simply blinked his chocolate eyes and bared his teeth as he attempted a disarming smile.

"I can help you, Señorita I know these vampires they're heathen to the bone -"

"My name is Ailana!"

I shouted, squirming helplessly. Two heavy pairs of shoes pounded the stairs and my front door flew open; Peter and Jameson appeared in the doorway, a raging mess of bloody fangs.

The third vampire rushed the two assailants in seconds. He flipped the larger vampire over his shoulder and threw him a good few feet, which ended in a booming crash as he collided with the fence separating mine from the neighbours.

Jameson' s face contorted into one of disgust. He was clearly bent on splattering my entrails all over the wall, but with his comrade sporting wood-inflicted injuries, he had no choice but to turn away and help him.

"Who are you?"

I asked. My saviour had his forehead leaned against the glass of the window, as I'd clambered into the driver's seat whilst no one could stop me.

"My name is Carlos, now will you have me in the car with you or not? I can protect you."

Screw it, I don't have time for this...

"Fine. Get in."

Carlos appeared in the seat next to me without warning, making me jolt in surprise.

Shaking myself, I chucked the gear stick into reverse and pressed the accelerator to the floor. His face was unreadable, poker straight.

"You're going to have to do some serious driving."

He warned.

As if I didn't know that already, fucking God damn-it.

"Just shut up and let me drive."

I growled, spinning the car off the drive like a mad woman and accelerated as soon as the gear stick clicked into place.

In the wing mirror I saw anger bubbling up on the faces of the two vampires, then they rapidly melted into the night and were gone.

Chapter Sixteen

I decided we would be safer travelling the narrow back roads lined with the silhouettes of ghostly, blacked out trees. It had stayed quiet. For a while.

"There appears to be someone behind us."

Carlos was pointing in the rear view; I checked the mirror and sure enough, another car was following at a steady pace. They'd crept up unnoticed until our bumpers were practically a hair's width apart.

Jameson sat in the driver's side wearing a smug grin, next to him was the brutish Peter who as I watched, opened his door and started to pull himself up onto the roof.

"For Christ sakes."

I muttered, hastily looking back at the road whilst I played with my locket. Carlos undid his seatbelt and brought down the window.

"What the hell are you *doing* mate?"

"I will require you to trust me Ailana, just keep your eyes on the road please. I am climbing out of the widow-"

"You *what*?"

"I believe Peter will attempt to jump onto our roof, I'm about to get in his way."

There were honestly no words I could think of in response. All I could do was grip the steering wheel like it was a life line, but really I was just scared of what would happen if I did anything else.

"Do a protection spell."

Carlos suggested, as he pulled his torso out of the car.

"I can't it's not as simple as that - hey - I'm not talking to my *flamin'* self am I?"

Carlos leapt like a panther onto the roof of their car, landing lightly on the balls of his feet and the tips of his fingers.

Despite his large body, Peter also had perfect balance. He brandished what looked like a wooden dagger; Carlos dodged the first attack, but on the second attempt he almost slipped from the roof.

My eyes swivelled from road to mirror, like I was watching some sort of horrific tennis match. When I was sure we weren't in danger of crashing, I checked on Carlos. Peter's hand was clamped tight around his arm as he stabbed his polished wooden dagger under Carlos' ribcage. He cried out in pain, then Peter tossed him from the roof in one, careless motion. Panicked, I yanked the steering wheel left and careered down a muddy verge.

Punching the breaks, I managed to bring my car to a stop centimetres off hurtling into a thick, gnarled tree. Quaking as my breath hitched in my throat, the sound of screeching tires on asphalt echoed through the night followed by deep, feral growls.

Coming to my senses I threw open the driver's side door; Jameson and Peter's car was parked precariously along the verge with its wheels poking over the edge. Peter crouched on top of the roof; he tucked his feet and legs underneath him ready to pounce.

I'm going to die.

I realised, which sparked a pang of misery in my gut. These vampires were going to kill me and that would be that. Carlos regained some sort of strength and used it to dive across Peter's path as he leapt towards my car.

In one blur of motion, he'd disarmed Peter and sliced his belly with his own weapon. Dark, congealed blood spattered over his already filthy boots and Jameson appeared at his man's side.

His face was arranged into one of serene calm, but his aura told a different story. In my mind's eye furious black waves seeped from Jameson's skin, like smoke from a fire.

"Carlos, you seem to have developed a habit for protecting and abetting these lower life forms. Give this silliness up, and she will die a quick death."

He purred, straightening his black jacket as if we were having a perfectly normal conversation.

"Who are you working for, why are you trying to kill this innocent girl?"

"That's hardly any concern of yours. I know you've been waiting a century or more to get a chance to kill me. I'm right here, why don't you take it?"

Carlos' nostrils flared, his eyes seemed to burn with a passion as old as the one Jameson talked about.

"Maybe not if it was I who put you in your grave first."

He added, as an after-thought. Peter watched from a distance; his face was screwed up in pain, one arm clutched his large belly whilst dark blood dripped to the ground. As they talked, a clear white light crossed the night sky, unseen by any of them.

I noticed it. I watched as the darkness morphed from faint grey into a soft pink. Right before it threatened to over take, I spoke.

"All of you will be in your grave if you don't shut up and make a damn decision."

The three of them looked towards the skyline becoming visible through the sparse trees; their faces dropped in horror.

"Jesus and Mary."

Jameson breathed, backing away from the sunlight that had come to devour them. Carlos started madly digging, leaving me to watch the vicious brothers sprint away.

Between them they shouldered their car and bounded up the verge, then they placed it back on the road with no more trouble than they would a child's toy.

By the time they'd sped off, Carlos had dug a six foot hole and was preparing to bury himself in it. I peered down into the Earth; its fresh smell was overwhelming yet surprisingly pleasant. He'd taken out a pen and a napkin from his pocket and was madly scribbling something down.

"Take this,"

He told me, holding out the napkin.

"Go and find my stash of blood bags, I will need them when I come out of here tonight if I'm to fend off any more attacks."

"They're not gonna stop until they get what they want."

"I will arise early tomorrow night, we can depart before those two have a chance to come back for us. You should make haste and gather together some spell ingredients, you will need them. It is imperative that you accomplish this before sundown and meet me back here."

I looked into his eyes, dark chocolate brown with only the reflection of the growing light of the sun in them. Despite my beliefs about his kind, Carlos had helped me, which was more than anyone else was doing.

"Do not fear the day ahead, Ailana. I'll be with you from dusk until dawn, for as long as it takes. I'll be damned if those two vile beings take another life of an innocent while I'm walking the Earth."

He vowed, now almost completely covered in dirt. I heaved the last few clumps of soil over the vampire's head; I had to remind myself that he was technically dead so of course, he wouldn't need to breathe under there.

"I'll be back for you."

I promised. My body was screaming at me for rest so I staggered back to my car, my mind reeling. I drifted into an uneasy sleep as the sun shone weakly on the horizon, the birds twittered like it was any other morning but of course, it was far from it.

Chapter Seventeen

I rang Aunt Helena five times when I woke up, only to hear her smooth voicemail tell me to leave a message each time.

The cheeriness of her recorded voice seemed to mock me, so I shoved my phone in my back pocket with a snort of annoyance. My whole body ached as I climbed out of the car to stretch my poor limbs; the sun had swept westwards while I slept and the clock on my dash told me it was half three.

I'd been asleep for nearly ten hours. Casting my eyes towards the spot where Carlos was buried, I saw the earth hadn't been touched.

I remembered the napkin he gave me with instructions for the task he'd set, though admittedly I found it crumbled and abandoned on the dashboard.

It was a sickening reminder that last night hadn't been a twisted dream or a terrifying nightmare - it was fucking real. I needed to get my ass in gear. Whilst traipsing up and down the edge of the narrow country lane, I managed to find some signal and called a taxi.

Though the sun shone weakly through a cloak of thin clouds, biting wind gnawed at my fingers turning them red. The journey was a blur, all I could think about was Jameson and Peter. When were they going to try and kill me again, and why did they want me dead so badly anyway?

Thankfully, the drive didn't take very long and we were soon back in Clee, where the trees alongside the road were replaced by houses, shops and people.

"Hey, we're 'ere luv."

The driver announced. I snapped out of a day dream filled with anxiety, grateful to be distracted.

"Thanks. Here's twenty quid, keep the change."

I mumbled, handing over the cash then hastily stepping out onto the high street.

A small number of people were still shopping up and down the promenade, but none of them looked happy. The wind shook sign posts and tousled hair, one unfortunate little boy even had his hot dog stolen by a seagull and started crying. I leaned against the wind, marching up a steep, hilled pavement until I found the B&B matching the address Carlos written down.

Nestled between a long line of other bed and breakfasts, I almost walked past it; two stories of awful lime green confronted me, coupled with a small wooden sign post painted pink, bearing the words 'Olive's Summer House'.

A young, thin woman with black hair sat at reception, staring unblinkingly at her computer screen. I showed her the napkin and asked which room belonged to a short man of Spanish origin, with strangely pale skin and a neat beard.

She handed me the keys with a look on her face, as if she thought I could do better. I guess despite his mannerisms and dress sense, this woman had been affected by the predatory vibes Carlos undoubtedly gave off - she was disturbed but she couldn't quite put her finger on it.

"What?"

I snapped, suddenly feeling protective over him. The woman shrugged and shook her head, turning away to pursue whatever she was looking at on the internet before I came in.

I ignored her, taking the keys to room 25 where on the balcony, I could see the Humber estuary stretched out like a divine, glistening blanket. The sun was nearing the horizon again now, it bounced off the waves so they twinkled at me from a distance.

It reminded me to get a move on; sunset was just around the corner. Carlos' room was unremarkable. A few smart shirts, trousers and belts hung on a black metal clothes rail, lined up underneath were a few pairs of pointed leather shoes.

A sizable leather trunk sat at the foot of a plain, wood framed bed, over which a few scanty sheets had been uncermoniously discarded.

Inside there was an eclectic mix of things, including a cooler with blood bags in it, which I grabbed.

I knew it would be wrong to look into the rest of his things, but I couldn't help myself. I started shifting stuff aside to look at what was underneath; a one hundred and fifty year old bottle of whiskey, a pack of cigars at least one hundred years old as well and a carnation in a glass bottle with a gold locket twisted around the neck.

Inside the delicate metal door was a faded picture of a woman, she had dark hair and large eyes the colour of almonds. The wind picked up outside and the front door creaked. I made myself jump and slammed the lid shut on the trunk, casting my eyes around in a panic.

Grey clouds gathered beyond the window; I felt that it was too lonely and too quiet. I looked at the cooler of blood bags I was holding with a little guilt; my family were more than sceptical about relationships with vampires.

How could so much change in a mere few hours? Heat travelled up my neck at an alarming rate while I thought, my blood pumped furiously almost breaking out of my veins. I clambered back down the stairs in a zombified stupor, all but throwing the room keys in the receptionist's face as I walked out.

My flat wasn't far from the B&B, so my feet carried me on autopilot while my mind churned over and over.

*

The same shitty mess I'd left before was there to greet me. Half the washing up was done, paperwork and DVD's littered every surface and empty pizza boxes were starting to smell. Tempted as I was to start cleaning, the fading light voted otherwise.

I only had a few minutes to change; I pulled on my jeans and shiny black boots with a sigh of relief, then threw on a red and black chequered shirt with a black cami-top. I then grabbed a shopping bag from under the sink and chucked in a few different vials of spell ingredients, snacks, a bottle of water and the blood bags.

Then came the trouble of finding Carlos' hiding spot. I called up a taxi and told the man who answered the phone, with welling eyes, that I'd lost my grandma's wedding ring on one of the backroads. We drove up and down, went back on ourselves a few times and eventually found the small stretch of messed up verge from the disastrous car journey the previous evening.

I signalled the taxi driver to stop and paid him to go on his way, thanking profusely.

Chapter Eighteen

Carlos climbed out of the dirt as the sun kissed the horizon between the trees. There was a chill in the air now as the coming night sapped the sun's warmth from the Earth.

I sat in my car with the door open so I could watch him. At first, what looked like a mole hill pushed its way through the dirt, followed by a grubby pale hand, then an arm and finally a dark haired head. I rushed over to help, taking Carlos' fingers which clamped onto mine like a steel vice.

With our combined efforts he pulled himself out of the dirt and lay against one of the thin tree trunks, exhausted.

"You look pretty rough ... How's the stab wound?"

I surreptitiously checked over the dark red stain on his shirt; the dried blood had turned black and crusty, but the wound itself had knitted back together and could've easily passed for a two week old injury.

"It is slowly healing, but I must have blood." He said, his voice rugged.

"Good thing I did what you asked then." I fished the blood bags out of the car and chucked them over. Carlos' eyes came alive as the plastic bags landed in his lap.

He snatched them up and ripped into the first one without hesitation. The veins under his eyes swelled with bloodlust, growing dark as he guzzled. I turned away with a creased brow, trying to keep in mind all he had done to help me stay alive.

"My first act as coven leader shouldn't be to run and hide, I should be the one protecting my family from these maniacs. Grandpa Maurice was killed by a vampire...I bet you anything it was those two. Now they're coming after me, his successor. The only thing I don't know is *why*."

"Your first act as Coven Leader, is it?"

Carlos asked, his eyebrow raised quizzically. The last few drops of blood had been drained from the bags, he pocketed them and stood so quickly he turned into a blur of drab colours.

"Well, I sort of ran away from a thing called The Lectio Ritu, it's a -"

"-Selection ritual for witches who's Coven leader has died, I have heard of it. I'm yet to have the pleasure of seeing you use magic, though."

I could've kicked myself for bringing it up, but I had no reason not to trust Carlos with the true story.

"Look, we need to get going." I said abruptly.

The dropping temperature became sharply apparent; the smell of wood bark and dirt permeated the air around us, creating a sense of unease.

"Can you do what Pete and James did yesterday? Can't you, like, lift the car back up onto the road or something?"

"Only if you promise to tell me more of this troubling coven business when we get going again."

Carlos replied, and I couldn't help but want to trust him.

"Okay fine, I'll tell you. Just please don't damage her."

I pleaded. Carlos rolled his eyes with a quiet chuckle.

"She is in good hands, but you might want to stand back, compadre."

He warned, and leaned down to lift the back bumper with one hand. I backed into a tree stump, nearly stumbled, then gained some footing and put an arm around another trunk behind it. Carlos reached underneath the car at the back, and lifted it onto his narrow shoulders.

"Jesus *Christ* mate."

I muttered, watching him drag the car carefully back onto the road. He spun the bumper round so the front would face the right way, afterwards he returned and offered me a piggy-back up the slope, which I accepted.

Carlos was in the driver's seat; we flew along the hodge-podge country lanes at ninety miles per hour, with the heating on full blast. I told him to make his way up to Whitby, and that I'd give him my aunt's address when we got closer. Carlos dug in his jacket and found a cigar.

He took a box of matches out and used one of them to light it; he puffed the acrid smoke all around us which made me cough, then he finally started the conversation again.

"So, you appear to be a witch on the run from her own coven. Would you care to explain how that happened?"

He asked.

"Can you open the window?"

"Oh, yes sorry."

Carlos cracked the window and I took a deep, grateful breath of clean air.

"The reason why I stopped practising magic is because I made a mistake that cost lives. I never want to make that mistake again."

I flinched, expecting him to be horrified at the prospect, as most people would be. But then I remembered he was a vampire, who'd probably seen more dead people than I'd ever met or ... something. He nodded, and took another deep toke on his cigar. This time he tipped a bit of ash out the window with his pinkie finger.

"Pray tell, what mistake was so terrible that you would shy away from who you are?"

He asked, keeping a steady eye on the road whilst puffing away.

"I suppose I can tell you since you saved my life yesterday, or whatever day it was. God, this staying up all night is really messing with my head."

I quietly sifted through the contents of my mind, almost losing myself in the memories until Carlos cleared his throat, bringing me back to the present.

"I was only five years old,"

I told him.

"My parents were both off work one weekend in the winter, near Christmas. Mum had gammon in the oven while she and my dad were busy upstairs, it was snowing heavily so we couldn't go out anywhere ... "

Rain lashed across the windscreen, driven by howling wind as we sped towards the North of Yorkshire. Silent tears dropped onto my lap; when Carlos placed a cold hand on my shoulder, I jolted in surprise. I know he meant to comfort me.

I wanted consolation - I needed it like I needed to breathe air - but it felt foreign and strange. Needless to say, I didn't know how to handle it at all.

"Do continue."

He encouraged gently, but his kindness only made me break down faster.

"I was bored, okay! I was trying to make the food cook quicker so I tried a spell I'd seen my mum do before and ... it all just ... caught fire. The whole house went up and only I escaped. After that, my aunt Helena came for me and I lived where we're headed to now for the next eighteen years. I decided to move back to Cleethorpes when I was old enough for college, I reconnected with some old friends and stuff like that. That's pretty much when I quit the coven - until grandpa Maurice was killed by those *flamin'* pair of wankers, anyway. I was called back to help them complete the ritual and wouldn't you know it, I'm bloody well chosen, 'ent I? You know everything else that's happened."

It was a minute before Carlos spoke again. He stubbed the cigar out and stowed away the last half of it in the inside pocket of his jacket. After taking a deep lungful of air, he turned to me.

"Here, wipe your eyes - "

He handed me a grubby handkerchief from his other pocket which I took, bypassing the gross factor in favour of dignity saved for later.

"Listen to me carefully, Ailana; your aura tells me how perfectly good your magic is. I can feel it pulsating next to me like electrified metal wire but you are afraid of it, why? What happened to your parents is in the past. It was a terrible, terrible accident and it was not your fault. I have witnessed so many vampires killing their own and vampires killing witches and witches and humans both killing each other and *blah, blah, blah*. I had to shut myself off, otherwise I would live my entire immortal life berating myself for all sorts of things. You have to let go of your past. You must raise a massive psychic boulder and throw it straight at your enemies! We are going to reach your aunt's mansion and make them aware of the danger, then your first act as Coven Leader won't be to let them die, but to unite them against a threat and lead them into victory! That story starts with you letting go of the past, accepting only that which you can control."

His words echoed in my head. They made perfect sense, but I couldn't help doubting myself. I'd been careful ever since that day and now, everything was different.

"Yeah but, what if-"

"No 'buts' no 'what ifs'. What happened before ... you were only a child. It was nought but an accident and it was out of your control. Now you have grown into adulthood you are in charge of your actions and your magic, you have the power to decide how they get used."

I noticed the distant glow of lights through the rain spattered glass. We were winding our way closer to a retail park with a few fast food restaurants, according to the signage on the side of the roads.

"I'm pretty hungry."

I mumbled as I thought it, and Carlos glanced my way with a smile.

"We can stop if you would like? Where do you normally prefer to dine?"

I had to hold back a laugh at the way he said 'prefer to dine'.

"Italian is my go-to, honestly. Spinach and ricotta pizza, pesto pasta, spaghetti and meatballs - you name it, I'm there."

"Should I go as far as to assume The Pizza House would suffice then?" He said evenly, to which I wholeheartedly agreed.

I'd been keeping my eye on the rear-view and so far, no other vehicles had caught up behind us. Carlos slowed the car and pulled into the next service stop; I closed my tired eyes and for the first time in a long time, I was able to completely empty my mind.

Chapter Nineteen

Stepping out into the cool air was a relief I never knew I needed. Now we were out of immediate danger, I closed my eyes and took a deep breath in. I focused on the wind, its subtle whistling and the sensation it created gently buffeting against my face, then I allowed my lungs to slowly empty.

The Italian restaurant was one of many dull, red brick retail buildings, surrounded by concrete roads lined with shrubs that seemed in want of some tender love and care. I clicked the button on my keys to lock the car before following Carlos inside.

It was nearly empty due to the late hour; only three or four tables were occupied. In a secluded corner booth was a family with two small, very well behaved children.

Another two couples occupied wooden tables in the room's centre and a tall, blonde woman on a laptop sat alone at the bar. I assumed she was the manager; her face was twisted into a mask of irritation whilst her fingers tapped furiously.

I looked away from the scene before me, letting the tension drain out of my body. I was desperate to forget the horrors I'd endured; the smell of cooking herbs, tomatoes and cheese made my stomach growl which replaced all images of vampires and witchcraft with the comforting thought of stuffing my face.

Carlos was able to get us seated and served almost instantly by hypnotising one of the waitresses; in no time at all I was heartily filling my boots with

BBQ pizza covered in chopped sausages, ham and chicken.

"This is well nice, thanks for bringing me." I said earnestly, to which Carlos gave a small nod of acknowledgment.

His arms were crossed against his chest and he kept looking towards the door. I'd have bet anything he was wondering how long it'd take James and Peter to catch up with us.

Personally, I was wondering how many years had passed since Carlos first came across them. Clearly they'd taken something dear to inspire such hatred, enough to last for over a century.

Who was the vampire that turned Carlos, what were they like? How many hundreds of years old were they, was it a man or woman? How did they manage to raise such a well mannered vampire, in a society that was surrounded by so much blood and death? More than anything, I thought it would be nice to get to know the man who had stuck by my side over the last couple of nights.

"When was the last time you saw your sire?" I asked. Carlos' thick eyebrows folded downwards as he thought about it.

"If I recall correctly it was nearly fifty something years ago." He replied after a moment.

"It was at the celebration of my hundredth year of immortality. He did his utmost to dissuade me from my quest to destroy Jameson and Peter, however I informed him there was nothing he could do to change my mind. I never did tell him my reasons for hunting them down ... "

"Would you tell me?"

Carlos paused for a moment as he thought, then he chuckled quietly.

"No but I will tell you this; Should I perish by their hands before our journey is concluded, there is a locket in my black trunk I request be given to Gillian. Furthermore, I would greatly appreciate it if my ashes could be scattered at The Sevilla Cathedral in Spain. Once Gillian receives the locket he will understand why I spent my immortality on two murderers who did not deserve it. He will be furious with me, but those feelings will surely fade."

"Why will he be furious?"

"Because Ailana, although he would have stood by my side no matter what, my reasons for the blood feud would be the cause of much controversy for him."

I couldn't help laughing freely; I leaned back in my chair and pushed myself away from the table with my foot, so my weight balanced on the back two chair legs, like I used to in school.

"I knew it! I knew you were a little wrong-un, I just knew it."

I joked, earning myself another, warm smile.

Carlos sipped his glass of whisky and I wiped my mouth on a napkin. With my plate clean and the waitress clearing the table, we paid and headed out to the car.

"Before we go on, there's something I'd like you to try."

Carlos announced. He strode ahead of me with his hands pocketed, clearly talking out loud to himself more than to me. I raised an eyebrow as the wind flew around us; it created an eerie howling through trees and disturbed the otherwise silent night.

"Like what?" I asked.

"I would like you to try a small protection spell, I think it would be well worth it and we need not make it complicated." He stated, to which I rolled my eyes.

"This again? I didn't think you were serious about that."

"Oh yes I'm er, how do the kids say it these days? 'Serious as cancer'."

I huffed irritably. What were the chances he would refuse to continue until I agreed to at least try? I thought, knowing that I really had no choice.

"Fine then," I said "where do you want to do this?"

"We'll continue on towards Whitby and stop at the first opportunity. Do you have the spell ingredients?"

"Yeah, I grabbed some when I went to mine. Let's get this over with."

I twiddled my necklace around my finger, facing away from Carlos as he pulled up in a dead end off road surrounded by green fields. The land was clothed in darkness and the weight of fear in my navel was almost suffocating. My throat and mouth were dry like the desert sands, my palms were sweating profusely as he parked and I clicked the light on above my head.

"Do not fear this Ailana, all you have to do is burn some herbs."

He said, watching as my unsteady hands attempted to untie the plastic bag holding the spell ingredients.

"Yes and write a sigil then light the candle, wait for the herbs to burn so I can seal them up - I know how it works."

I snapped.

He was only trying to make me feel better - I knew that - but I was overwhelmed and quickly getting irritated.

"Sorry, I just can't-"

"Allow me."

Carlos took the bag and ripped a hole in it, then handed it back with a smile.

"Okay, now I feel stupid."

I said sheepishly, earning myself a playful chuckle. When the fresh scent of sage wafted into the enclosed space, so too did the pain of nostalgia. I fought to push the memories aside so I could focus; Carlos fell silent as I worked, carving sigils into the candle wax to ward off those who would do us harm. I drew a circle of herbs and salt then placed the sage, basil and bay leaves on a charcoal disc on top of a square of tinfoil.

Finally, I took a shaky breath and drew the flames onto the herbs and candle. They flickered and sparked, crackled and popped - it was mesmerising to watch. Within minutes a relaxing wave spread over us, my eyelids drooped lazily and Carlos' rigid pose melted into a relaxed slump much like my own.

We sat quietly while the embers burned, listening to the rain bouncing off the car roof. Smoke spirals twisted and flowed out of the slightly cracked window, once it died down I snuffed the candle flame and broke the circle, which I swept back into the bag along with everything else.

"The air feels different, for sure."

Carlos murmured, wafting his hand through the smoke still lingering around us.

"Alright," I said nervously "Let's get going."

The 'going' bit never came.

An ear splitting screech of metal being torn apart erupted above our heads; the roof was peeled back like the lid of a tuna can to reveal my worst nightmare, leering over us as rain spattered into the car.

Before we could react, Peter's hand shot down like a speeding arrow and yanked Carlos out of his seat.

I wanted to scream, but instead I kicked my brain into gear and opened the car door, though a sad little voice inside reminded me there wasn't a chance in hell I'd be able to outrun the vampires.

Jameson's callous laugh sounded behind me as I stumbled on the wet grass; I caught sight of their car parked only a short distance away. if I could only reach it, there might be a chance to escape. Jameson closed the distance between us faster than a bolt of lighting.

A scream ripped free of my lungs as he grabbed my arm with enough force to crack the bones. Splinters tore into muscle as Jameson shattered my humerus under his titanium grip.

His face was clean of blood now it was dripping with rain water; loose strands of dirty blonde hair were plastered to his face, but his evil eyes glowed bright with hatred.

Looking into those eyes was akin to looking down a gaping chasm at the top of a mountain, inside which bubbling pits of lava were waiting to be unleashed on the world.

"You surmised that you could ward us off with something so pathetic and elementary as a simple protection spell?"

He said, his usually smooth voice came out as a deep growl.

"You are every bit as weak as ever you thought you were, witch."

Grunts of pain sounded behind me as Carlos and Peter struggled; my inner voice demanded I turn around and look to make sure my friend was okay, but I couldn't take my eyes off Jameson.

In the moment between his deciding whether to kill me or to prolong the torture, a sharp snap echoed in the night around us. Carlos' grunts ceased and I knew he'd just had his neck broken.

"You *fucker*!"

Jameson's smile returned with a vengeance; he made to breeze past but I clamped my good hand onto his jacket sleeve. He glanced down at it with an amused expression, then turned his hawk eyes on mine.

"If you wish to see this dire excuse for a vampire again before we kill him, or indeed, if you wish to see any of your family members before you die, meet us at Helena's mansion within the next two hours."

Jameson shook his arm free as Peter threw Carlos' lifeless body over his shoulder. They disappeared from sight; I barely had seconds to get into my own car before I lost them. They sped off as I stuck the keys in the ignition and threw the car in reverse.

I punched the accelerator and slammed the door shut only when I'd taken off. My car was nowhere near fast enough, I couldn't even read the number plate in front going at seventy five.

After a short distance lights appeared in my peripheral vision and steadily grew brighter; a train track up ahead had lowered its barriers, the train was visible through the sparse trees lining the tracks, hurtling in our direction at a ferocious speed.

Oh wait, you're kidding - they're not gonna do what I think they are - are they?

A line of three cars were waiting in front of the barrier. Jameson tugged at the wheel of his vehicle and veered sharply to the right in the nick of time, avoiding a collision with the back of a silver saloon.

He didn't stop there. He smashed through both sets of barriers. I stomped on my breaks, heart filled with despair as his bumper disappeared from sight on the other side, seconds before the train breezed past. My heart was racing; I realised I was holding my breath as I watched the train whizz past, so I sucked in a lungful of air and then another, and another until I was hyperventilating.

My left arm was throbbing with unbelievable pain; gritting my teeth, I reached for my phone with the other and dialled my aunt Helena once more.

It went straight to voicemail. Fat tears rolled down my cheeks alongside the rain splattering through the giant hole I now had in my roof. Aunt Helena's recorded voice told me to leave a message after the beep.

"Auntie, it's Ailana. I need you to lock all your doors right now, don't let anyone in. You're not safe. The vampires that broke into your house last time, the ones that killed grandpa Maurice, they're coming for you. But so am I, I'll be there as soon as I can. I love you."

I ended the call and threw my phone on the passenger seat. The smashed barriers were now lifting to let cars through again; they navigated the debris Jameson and Peter had left behind and I followed them, overtaking at the first chance I got.

Chapter Twenty

All I could imagine was my aunt and cousin, torn to shreds, and me arriving too late to find their faces blank and their eyes staring. My hands slipped on the steering wheel, slick with sweat. I wiped silent tears of frustration from my cheeks, reminded constantly of my injured upper arm, which had turned purple and black and throbbed painfully.

I drove along the lonely winding roads in the darkness, unaware of my actions; I couldn't face the thought of not getting there in time. I decided it was time to screw the speed limit, and put the pedal to the metal. Carlos had opened my eyes to a new reality, he'd protected me and been a true friend in the short time we'd spent together. He'd believed in my magic - even saved me from certain death - it was my duty to save him now the tables were turned.

The signage for Whitby was soon illuminated in my car headlights; most of the narrow, cobbled roads and paths were gripped by deathly silence. The town's residents were sleeping safe and sound, unaware of the danger in their midst. Familiar, quaint old buildings lined the streets, stacked up behind each other along the hilly landscape and coming to a head at the docks.

Fishing boats and private yachts floated next to each other on the glistening, still water as it reflected the moonlight. Crab nets were stacked one on top of the other on the concrete ground and a few seagulls were circling overhead.

Helena's mansion was visible a short distance away from the crumbling old Abbey; I flung myself around each corner, actually leaving the road at one point as I *zoomed* over a bump and landed a moment later.

After a while, I was forced to slow my speed due to the lack of street lamps; I inched my car through crowded, six foot tall bushes either side of the road until I reached Helena's front gate. My tires finally crunched to a stop on the gravel driveway in front of my old family home.

Jameson and Peter had left the front gates wide open, and their car was parked at an angle in the middle of them. With shaking palms, I pulled out the car keys and ran to inspect the vehicle. The doors stood open, and a pool of black liquid slowly leaked out of the passenger's side, dripping in a curving line towards the house.

A moment passed before it dawned on me; the liquid was the remnant of what Carlos had consumed from the bags I bought him, blood that had been running in his own veins, blood which was now wasted on the gravel driveway. He was hurt badly; a distant wail sounded from somewhere within the mansion.

I sucked in a deep breath as relief flooded my body; there was still time. My left arm still twinged painfully. After a moment of deliberation I crouched down at the pool of blood and dipped two fingers into it.

I squeezed my eyes shut as I brought them to my lips, ready to steel myself against the vile taste. A surprisingly sweet flavour trickled over my tongue; the moment it flushed down my throat my bones and muscles began to mend.

In a matter of seconds, the bruises disappeared and the bones cracked back into place. My torn muscles repaired themselves and I sighed with relief as the pain dissipated. There was no time to be in awe of the fact. I abandoned the car park and sprinted towards the front door, which had also been left wide open. Bright light flooded out of the entrance hall, momentarily blinding me.

"Aunt Helena?"

I called, my eyes darting around pristine red painted walls and gold gilding along the staircase, looking for any signs that would suggest a struggle.

"Kitty?"

The only sound that issued in turn was the pained cries echoing from somewhere below.

They're in the wine cellar...

I realised. Desperation gripped me like a crushing serpent; I made a beeline for the wooden hatch in the kitchen floor. Unclasping the latch, I heaved the thick lid of wood up and over; blackness cloaked the concrete steps leading down there.

With no access to a light switch, I turned on my phone torch and descended the steep stairs which led to a subterranean, freezing room full of barrels, kegs and wooden crates, each peppered with dust. It was a large space, but made to look smaller by the amount of product that was in there.

"Carlos? It's me!"

I hissed, swinging my phone around, hoping and dreading what it's beaming light would find.

Muffled cries sounded from one of the corners and I jerked in its direction. Carlos was tied to a wooden chair, gagged and bleeding.

It was a wonder that he could keep his head up, let alone cry out. I rushed over and pulled off the blue cloth that had been viciously wrapped around his mouth.

"Ailana......you must......you must leave."

His dark pupils rolled in his head, his skin was paler than ever, tinted green around the underside of his eyes. The sticky black blood I'd found outside was still oozing from his neck.

It looked as if either James or Pete had gone to town on him with their teeth. I attempted to hastily untie the ropes that bound his arms around the back of the chair.

"They're soaked in some kind of binding potion, I cannot escape without the help of a witch."

He told me; his voice was ragged and low, showing the pain and effort it took just to speak to me.

"It's your lucky day then, innit?"

I replied evenly, though I didn't feel lucky in the slightest.

"You need blood, you can drink mine but you need to be quick-"

"Ailana you don't.....understand, it's not...."

He trailed off; his head lolled over his chest in a disturbing, unnatural way.

"Carlos we don't have *time* mate! I've got to save my family from those psychos so drink up and get on with it."

I shoved my wrist in his mouth without waiting for a reply and felt his jaws crush down on my bones. Four, needle-like stabs into my veins made me gasp. I felt dizzy. It didn't take long for my legs to get pins and needles, but before I could black out the pain stopped.

Carlos pulled away with a feral growl; I grabbed the chair for momentary support, watching as my blood healed his wounds, then I went back to work feverishly on the ropes.

"Carlos, I think I'm nearly do-AHHH!"

From out of nowhere a hand grabbed me, jerked backwards and sent me crashing into a pile of boxes. Bottles of wine smashed around my body and their scattered shards dug painfully into my back. I wailed in pain as Jameson stood over me, his eyes alive with malice and greed above flaring nostrils, while fresh blood poured from the wounds in my back.

"Why are you doing this?"

I squeaked, unable to think of anything else. He scrunched his face up into a mock wounded expression.

"*Why are we doing this*? So that my clan can finally lay hands on a spell which would enable us to walk in the sun, that's why. And I will not be allowing a frail, pathetic teenage witch to get in my way."

Without warning, Jameson grabbed my arm and yanked me forward; the reeking smell of rotten meat clouded his breath, flecks of tinged red spittle oozed in the corners of his mouth. His eyes were wide, unblinking - he looked insane.

He opened his mouth wide, his fangs glinted in what little light there was and I knew within moments, they would pierce my skin. Behind us, Carlos had freed himself from his prison and now came at Jameson like a bullet train.

He grabbed the other vampire by his throat, locked his fingers on and threw the man down with such force that his head made a crater in the concrete floor.

He was up in almost an instant, a snarl twisted his features but what was more; the gruesome sight of his crushed head steadily knitting back together in front of my eyes. The flesh crept over the bone, cracking sounds came from his skull as it mended and smoothed back out. I shrunk into myself, unable to move any further back.

"I've entertained this insufferable song and dance for a century too long! I'm ending this."

Jameson growled, crouched low and ready to pounce.

Carlos mirrored his stance, then jumped - too early to see the wooden dagger he'd pulled out of his pocket. It was finely carved and glossy with varnish, the tip was sharp enough to slice through anything - dead *or* alive.

Jameson swung the weapon in an arc and slashed Carlos across the face, missing his throat by inches. He threw Carlos bodily into a stack of steel kegs; the klang of abused metal muffled his cry of pain, but he was straight back up and caught Jameson speeding towards him. For a few minutes they were a blur, toppling each other into walls and boxes at supernatural speed.

It was impossible to tell who was who, but Carlos managed to get Jameson on his back and pinned under his knee, now clutching the dagger in his own hand.

"Adiós, engendro del diablo. Esto es para Maria!"

Carlos said, then he plunged the wooden dagger into Jameson's heart.

The vampire's screams died almost the second they rose; his body was solid one moment, then it disintegrated into a pile of grey and white ash at Carlos' feet.

"YOU!"

A voice boomed; all the commotion had drawn the attention of James' minion. His large body blocked the light flooding the staircase, but he was as graceful on his feet, like a cat stalking a cornered mouse. Carlos wasn't quick enough to stop Peter from barreling into him; he flew backwards through the air and knocked several bottles of wine off a shelf.

They shattered spectacularly on the floor, and in the second before Peter charged again, Carlos was ogling at them as if he'd never seen smashed bottles before. He grabbed a jagged piece of glass and held it in front of him like a sword, jagged points stretched out towards his enemy.

Carlos swung his arm round like a pro baseball player on steroids. He timed the blow just right so that Peter had no way of avoiding it. The lethal glass sliced right through Peter's neck, severing it all the way across. For one precarious moment, Peter's body wobbled where he stood, then his head toppled off and the body slumped with a thud after it.

"What the *fuck*! Oh that's so disgusti-*Uuugh...*"

I threw up before I could finish the sentence.

"Ailana are you alright? Let me see your wounds,"

Carlos rushed over to lift me up and started pulling the glass out of my back.

"Listen, I have to tell you something you will not like, I only have a moment-"

"You don't even have that."

A third voice sounded from the stairwell, a familiar one with deep, rippling undertones of honey.

"Auntie Helena?"

I guessed, unable to turn and look for myself.

"Yes dear, it's me." She replied.

"You venomous - "

Carlos had started to say, until a sudden force of wind flew about the place; it lifted him from the ground so he was suspended in the air above us.

"Auntie he's been helping me, he's not like the other two!"

I assured her, but she just smiled serenely as she clacked across the floor in her expensive heels towards the vampire.

"Oh, I know. Those buffoons were gullible enough to believe I would give them a spell to walk in the sunlight, for helping me. This one wasn't. I offered him half a million pounds to turn against you, earlier tonight and he refused."

Helena took Jameson's dagger from Carlos, and studied it in what little light was available.

"They *did* know how to whittle though, I'll give them that..."

She muttered. Maybe I'd banged my head one too many times and I was confused. It sounded as if Helena was telling me she was behind the attacks.

"What the hell is happening?" I asked.

"Ailana,"

Carlos called to me

"-remember, *you* are in charge of your magic, you must *use* it!"

Helena tutted, as if his words were some annoying buzzing sound that needed to be quelled.

"That's enough of you!"

She snapped, punching him twice in the heart with the dagger. She dropped the winds, and Carlos fell to the floor. His body crumbled to a pile of ashes upon impact.

Chapter Twenty One

I tried to scream, but I couldn't breathe. My heart felt like it had been ripped open, as waves of shock wracked my body. He was gone, Carlos was really gone.

"What the *hell* auntie! You've lost it, you've completely lost it!"

Hot splashes landed on my cheeks, and my face grew hot with emotion. Carlos was dead and all this time, my aunt had been plotting to kill me.

"What's *wrong* with you?"

I shouted between hitched breaths, unable to tear my gaze away from the sorry lump of ashes that used to be my friend.

"Darling, what's wrong with *you*? You only serve to embarrass my family's bloodline with your hulu magic - that you can't even perform - might I add. It would be fraudulent to even call you a witch, really. As for those two pathetic leeches, they would've drained me of every last drop of blood in my body, routine predatory opportunity and all that. But I didn't want to die, I have plans to put into action you see and so I made them a deal; my coven leader's life for mine. They happily agreed to kill my father, a great loss on my part but I assure you, it had to be done. I assumed everything would be as it needed to be afterward, that I would ascend and become an elder in the wider magical community."

As she spoke a dark look came over my aunt's face; it was an ugly look that twisted her features and sapped away all the niceness that might've been there.

"And then you were picked, of all people." She continued, rolling her eyes dramatically.

"I was...so insulted that my own father, first, would choose Elliot over me but then *you*? Did you know he nearly died of a heart attack, my father? Years ago I heard them discussing Elliot's ascension at dad's bedside. Obviously he recovered, though I'd already decided your father had to go or it would be him instead of me."

My stomach turned over then, I wretched but nothing but dryness caught in my throat.

"My dad,"

I said, between laboured breaths.

"You were going to *kill my dad*?"

"Not 'were going to', 'did'."

Helena's smile grew with my horror.

"Yes, it was me who started that fire, not you. I was spying at the time, when you were attempting to expedite the cooking of christmas dinner using spells, and I suddenly realised the whole situation was perfect; a scapegoat, a blameless tragic accident caused by an infant. It was almost too good to be true."

The words she spoke seeped under my skin like black mould, just as the toxins from a spider bite slowly winds towards its victim's heart. The heat in my body doubled, intensified with rage. When my skin started breaking out in hives I knew it was because of her; Helena had fooled me and my entire family with her schemes for years and now people I cared about were dead, including a vampire I'd thought was immune to such heartless destruction.

And perhaps the most important deception of all...my parents didn't die because of me. I pushed myself off the ground and reached behind my back; shards of glass were still lodged beneath my shoulder blades. I ripped them out with a scream of agony, and discarded them on the floor.

"You don't know me, you have no idea what I'm capable of. That vampire you just killed? He knew me better than you in three days."

Helena's face contorted into a spiteful mask. Her eyes turned to slits. They shone malignantly and I kicked myself internally for not noticing it sooner.

"Mum, Aila...what's going on?"

A voice sounded from the stairway.

Kitty had been drawn by all the screams and shouts; I could tell from her pink silk pyjamas and half glued eyes that she'd just got out of bed.

Helena's face turned ghostly pale.

"Kitty, get back upstairs!"

She snapped, the fear apparent in her shaking voice. Guilt tore me apart when I looked over at my cousin, who was just as confused as I felt. Kitty ignored her mum, instead she stepped further into the room.

"What in *helheim* is going on down here?"

She demanded, her voice a shrill tone that rang in my ears and in my head. She looked from me - covered in cuts and blood - to her Mum who was still holding the dagger.

"She didn't know about any of this, did she?"

I exclaimed, looking back at Helena, who snarled sadistically. Within seconds, whatever response that'd been on her lips, died. Her face melted into a look of horror, eyes wide and mouth slack.

The heat in my body grew while she was talking, the heat amplified in exact correlation with the garbage spewing out of her mouth. Tiny sparks erupted from my skin, at first only one or two, then they morphed into fully fledged flames coursing up and down my arms like crashing waves on the ocean.

"Cuz, I think you'd better leave."

I warned, but she didn't budge. Kitty was immobilised by the stairs, now cowering in fear with her hands on either side of the wall for support.

Helena jumped at the chance to strike while I wasn't looking.

She raised both her arms as if to embrace the grungy ceiling lamps; at first there was a faint rumble, then chunks flew out of the brick wall on both sides of the room with a resounding BOOM!

Kitty's scream pierced the air. I ducked low as thin vines covered in thorns shot through the holes - speeding towards me with killer accuracy.

I flung my arms out in front of me like a fiery shield, keeping my head bent low. The vines struck my wrists but there was barely a moment of pain; I thought of Carlos' words while tendrils wound themselves around me.

You have to let go of your past. You must raise a massive psychic boulder and throw it straight at your enemies!

I twisted my hands up and round to get a better grip on the vines. Closing my eyes, I focused.

Stronger...

I thought.

Much stronger...

The vines hardened between the tingling heat glowing in my palms; When I opened my eyes, I saw glinting titanium chains. I yanked towards me and they broke away from the ancient brickwork.

Helena only had time to glare; I whipped the chains up and around - towards her. She dived sideways at the last minute and the metal clanged off a stack of wooden crates, sending them crashing down.

She rolled over and slammed her hand on the concrete. From her fingertips a blast of cold air and ice gushed over the grimy floor, twisting my way like a giant snake.

I brought my hands together in front of my body, remembering the energy summoning techniques my mother used to show me.

"Kāhea wau i ke akua 'o Ku, lawe mai ahi!"

I shouted, flinging my own arms up to the sky. The ground grew hot under my feet whilst flames erupted in a blazing circle around me; it chased the ice down until it melted over the floor.

Water lapped against the broken boxes and bottles in the aftermath of my power surge, as Helena groggily pushed herself up from the ground, having been knocked down yet again in the assault.

The flames died like wind suddenly dropping mid-howl. Her ginger hair hung in limp clumps down her back; it stuck to her face so that her usual, striking appearance was gone; replaced by a scowling, drenched hag with running mascara.

"Give it up Helena, I'm not letting you destroy me or this coven."

We both panted for breath; sweat dripped over my lips and out of my hair, over my eyes, blinding me.

My aunt was panting heavily, shaking as she balanced with her hands on her knees. Her green eyes found my brown ones; each reflected hatred for the other, each searching for any sign of weakness, a chink in the other's armour.

"Dominus belli -"

Helena began, in rasping, low tones that shook me to the bone marrow.

"- comminuet montem."

"No wait, mother, you don't have to do this, Ailana can pardon you!" But even Kitty's desperate cries for rationality had no effect on her.

"Dominus belli, comminuet montem."

Above, a rumbling and cracking sounded, loose pieces of rock and stone broke and shook over us in a cloud of dust.

"No way, no! There's no way she's getting pardoned - the best you can hope for is becoming an outcast!" I shouted, as the rumbling grew louder, the ceiling shook violently - we would be crushed within minutes.

"Dominus belli -"

"Helena!" I screamed.

"- comminuet montem!"

I dived out the way as a large chunk of rock broke above my head. I landed somewhere near Kitty's feet; our arms grabbed around each other for a moment, then she pulled me up and we looked over the destruction. Helena was trying to crush me to death; the only problem was, her daughter was in there with us.

"Kitty, get outside I'll be right behind you."

I ordered, but still she struggled against me.

"What about my mum?"

She wailed, though Helena's eyes were dark around the edges. Moisture welled up in the corners of Kitty's eyes; she could see the truth in front of her, but her mind didn't want to accept it.

I suppose anyone would prefer to remain ignorant in the case of a family member's failure, it was no different than my refusal to practise magic after the fire in the snow, where my parents were taken from me forever. In the end we all have to come to our senses; we have to do what's right, not what's easy.

"Kitty please let's *go*!"

I shouted; my heart shattered all over again when I stared into her desperate, scared face. As she suppressed a sob and turned away, I wasted no time dragging her up the stairs. The whole property was shaking now; centuries old foundations quaked around us as the hull of a ship rocks from side to side in a storm.

I was running without thinking, my lungs were bursting from the adrenaline in my blood. The only thing that kept my feet on the ground was my cousin's warm hand in mine, and our noisy breath pounding in and out of our lungs.

We cleared the kitchen and hallway, soon we were pounding over the cobbled driveway towards the gates while cold rain lashed at our skin.

A great sigh came from the mansion; we turned when we reached the gate in time to see the ground swallowing up our home. The fine towers tumbled onto the courtyard below with a resounding, explosive crash.

After what seemed like forever the grinding of earth stopped; the rubble and dust settled and soon only the jagged, skeletal remains of broken stone could be seen, struck against the sky as light slowly infected the dark. The house was a worn and helpless caricature of its once glorious self.

Tears ran anew over my cheeks. I wondered why my fingers felt cold; it was only then that I realised I was squeezing Kitty's hand to death, and she was crushing the life out of mine.

Neither of us spoke for a very long time; we sat on the hard gravel in the rain which delicately toppled down over us. We held each other for ages, at times sniffling and at others we were unable to stop the tears.

Soon dawn touched the land on the eastern horizon, I'd managed to convince Kitty to get up and into my car, where although the roof had been torn off, she could sleep more comfortably for the time being.

I climbed in the driver's side next to my cousin; her chest rose and deflated in a calm rhythm, giving the illusion of peace, but I could see pain etched in her face as she slept.

I watched the sky for a bit longer. The sun rose higher, but the pain in my chest only worsened. I would never wait for Carlos to emerge from the dirt at dusk again, I would never ring my Aunt Helena to check in.

We would never be the same after that night.

Chapter Twenty Two

Relentless sun bore down on the ancient cathedral; she was an old friend, and like most good friends she'd turned a blind eye to the destruction and ruin in my wake.

She cast her rays through a thin veil of clouds onto leviathan walls of intricate, gothic design. The courtyard stemmed from one of the cathedral's chambers, and it was surrounded by a square ring of sapling orange trees.

Kitty hadn't said a word to me once we left the hotel room that morning. The pain of getting up and facing the day was written clearly on her face, but each time she caught me looking she would smile; as if I'd let the suffering of my cousin go.

Her hair wasn't meticulously styled, nor did it tumble over her shoulders like a cascading waterfall of shining bronze. She'd simply parted it down the middle and tied it back with a plain hairband. It wasn't like my Kitty.

"When Carlos told me he wanted his ashes scattered in the Seville Cathedral, I never thought I'd be the one doing it."

I told her, in a feeble attempt to get her talking about something, but she just nodded. She was hurting real bad, but as much as felt for her I couldn't get too caught up in her grief. Aunt Helena may have been her mother, but she tried to kill me. She'd also killed one of my friends and our Grandpa; there was only so far my sympathy could stretch.

"I've never been to this part of Spain before, it's beautiful."

She managed after a while.

"It's far too busy for my liking though, I try to avoid crowds of non-magic folk if I can help it."

"Kitty!"

"What? I'm just being honest."

I rolled my eyes at the sky and smiled a little.

"I suppose you're right. Let's do this then, before I lose my nerve."

I held up the urn and Kitty nodded, taking a step back. My sweating hands slipped on the lid; after a moment of pathetic struggling I opened the container and poured the contents into the great, stone water-fountain that dominated the courtyard of orange trees. I looked at Kitty.

"Are you ready?"

I asked. She nodded firmly. We both crouched down holding hands, then recited the incantation in barely more than a whisper.

"Everlasting flower grow, with tears of sorrow sow, lest he be forgotten, this love he hath begotten."

Keeping Kitty's hand in one, with the other I reached into my pocket and brought out some hemp and poppy seeds. I threw them in the water like I did with the ashes, then we stood up and waited.

Within minutes, a small clump of red flowers pushed their way through the crack of the paving stone that bordered the fountain.

"It's Bishop of Llandaff."

I breathed, recognising the black stem and the dark reddish leaves.

"I'm sorry?"

"Bishop of Llandaff, it's a type of dahlia."

I explained, admiring its delicate, showy flower heads. My cousin sat down on the fountain's edge in quiet contemplation, so I joined her.

"Will you be going to mum's funeral?"

She asked eventually, fiddling with the hem of her skirt instead of looking at me.

"I'm actually planning to get a flight to Hawaii from here, I'm not going back to England for a while."

I explained, expecting her to be at least a little shocked. Her expression hardly shifted, making it hard to tell how she was really feeling which I guess was how she wanted it.

"You're going to your mum's family in Kohala, then." She guessed, staring avidly at the hem of her skirt.

"Yes ... I was actually going to ask if you'd like to take over as Coven Leader until I return? I know it's what your mum wanted for you."

The truth of it was hard to digest; we both remembered back to the horror Helena created to get Kitty in my position.

She ran her fingers through her hair with a furrowed brow as she mulled the offer over. She smiled somewhat hesitantly, then after a few minutes, she held a hand out for me to shake.

"I'll do it."

I swatted her hand away and pulled her in for a hug.

"Thank-you."

I murmured into her hair. We stayed that way for a long time, just holding each other. We sat for a little while longer, then Kitty called herself a taxi to take her back to the hotel.

"Aren't you coming?"

She asked, looking over her shoulder to see me standing back on the pavement. I waved her on, then leaned down to whisper in her ear when she was sitting comfortably.

"I have one last vampire to deal with first, I'll see you in the morning."

I had time to see her face blanch at the mention of vampires, but I swung the door shut before she could try to convince me to go with her.

The driver pulled off and I watched the taxi disappear from sight.

*

When night deigned to grace the plaza with its shadowy charm, spotlights beamed in the sun's place; they illuminated an arc of still water that ran in a semi-circle around the old platform.

A regal fountain took centre stage, its gushing water creating a symphony of calm as it echoed off the walls of the surrounding buildings. I focused on its rhythm and breathed deeply, then after a few minutes my heart rate slowed its hammering on my ribcage. I'd skimmed over some lengthy descriptions of the vampire I was meeting in Carlos' journals; apparently he could drown an entire room out with his hearty laugh and his wide, white toothed smile.

I couldn't bring myself to snoop so deeply into Carlos' things when I recovered his belongings from the motel, a dignity I'd regretted giving as I waited for the man who'd made him.

I paced up and down the plaza, over and again until I felt like giving up; that's when I heard a voice sing like jingle bells in the darkness. The vampire appeared behind me without so much as a pair of footsteps.

"The only time I've ever seen someone pace like you this evening was in a boardroom in New York ... and London and Singapore and Switzerland. And Montreal, but I won't tell you that wild story until we're better acquainted. Anyway, I've been watching you for a good several minutes from the shadows, I hear the clink of a metal chain in your pocket which means you have something to give me."

His voice was deep and rugged, but gregarious enough to put me at ease almost instantly.

I turned towards the sound to put a face to the epic monologue. I was standing head to pecs with a man of six foot something, his broad shoulders and chest were adorned in a frilled blouse and a long, formal coat of deep maroon, embroidered with gold stitching woven into a regal pattern of swirls. He had to be the first bloke I'd ever seen wearing knee high boots - almost thigh highs - over a pair of cream coloured, skin tight trousers.

His teeth and two pairs of non-retractable canines - top and bottom - each glowed whiter than the moon herself. His grin was so big it dominated his strong, pale face which - along with a thin covering of dark fuzz over his cheekbones and jawline - went very easy on the eye.

Shoulder length hair fell in loose brown curls and his murky green eyes were overshadowed by thick, dark eyebrows.

For some reason I couldn't let go of the locket, though the burly, enthusiastic vampire had his hand outstretched, waiting for me.

"How old are you?"

The words were out before I could stop myself, but the reaction I expected didn't come.

The vampire simply stared at me nonplussed, then he threw his head back and laughed. He laughed so loud I was afraid every person in Sevilla would hear him.

"It's a pleasure to meet you too. My name is Gillian Roberts and I am, in fact, five thousand years old."

I tried not to gape, but I couldn't help it.

Where are your bloody manners?

My inner voice scolded.

I dunno, but I bet they're having more fun than I am...

I thought defiantly. I straightened my back and punched my chin up so I could look at him full on.

"I'm Ailana Highstone and er, it's nice to meet you, as well. Basically, Carlos saved my life from these two psychopaths and he told me you'd understand why he was hunting them if I gave you this."

I explained, pulling it out for him to see. He seemed to recognise the simple gold chain; his brow creased for half a second, then his face became a smooth, unreadable mask.

"According to what you told me over the telephone, Carlos has passed and you wish to scatter his ashes at the cathedral."

"My cousin and I already did that. We had to do it during the day, it's the easiest way to get in."

"What of the rest of his belongings?"

"The trunk and his clothes and stuff are in my hotel room, it's only a few blocks away from here. You could walk there with me, then we'll say our goodbyes."

I held the necklace out and Gillian took it; when he opened the locket's little doors his expression changed. Anger crossed him, then frustration then calm again.

"Goddamn it, Carlos."

He muttered, closing his eyes as he held it crushed against his chest. I didn't know what to say or what any of it meant, so I waited in silence until his eyes flickered and he remembered I was there.

"He never did forget about her." The vampire said, in mysterious tones.

"Never forgot about who?"

He raised an eyebrow, almost mocking my lack of knowledge.

"There is a time and a place for stories, in the dinner halls of one of my many fine establishments where I ensure my guests are watered and fed. Only after asking their express permission to drink their blood will I then share the tales of grand adventures past. However, I sense you have something else on your mind at this moment?"

He was right. I hadn't planned on being waylaid by a five thousand year old philanthropist on my way to Hawaii, but I was too curious to say no.

"I'm supposed to catch a flight tomorrow, my cousin's waiting at the hotel - "

"Then by all means, invite her along. I have a wonderful state of the art mansion on the banks of the guadalquivir, unfortunately I must refuse to discuss anything with you until we are inside its walls. Forgive me, but I haven't met many witches who would deign to consort with vampires - I am moved by your efforts to ensure Carlos reached his desired final resting place. Won't you indulge an old man, accompany me home so I may tell you of how my young friend came to be in your defence to begin with?"

At that moment, the moon was full and shining over the whole plaza. I knew it would be shining over Hawaii as well, where my maternal family would be waiting. I decided they could wait a little longer. I took the vampire's proffered elbow, and allowed myself to be escorted away into the night.

THE END

Printed in Great Britain
by Amazon